The Ex-mas Breakup

a Pine Harbour Christmas novel

Zoe York

A booty call with your ex? Bad decision, Rory.

I really thought it would be a one-time thing. A hormonal moment of weakness where I text him a funny ha-ha realization that I'm ovulating and he knows what that means—I can't turn my brain off. He used to be so good at helping with that...

Then Garrett shows up *very* quickly. Bickering leads to banging, and it's better than ever, raw and real and super satisfying. So maybe we didn't work out as a couple, but "exes with benefits" has a nice ring to it, at least until I finish my residency. Just once a month.

A Christmas road trip? Disaster ahead, Garrett.

I know I messed up when I broke Rory's heart eight months ago. I also know we can't spend more than ninety minutes together without everything crumbling, and the drive back to Pine Harbour is six times that long. Too bad leaving Rory behind—or for good—just isn't an option. Whether she likes it or not, I'm her guy. Her ride home.

Which means when we arrive at her parents' Christmas tree farm and discover her sister in tears over a breakup of her own, and Rory takes one pleading look at me... Suddenly I'm her "boyfriend" again.

And there's only one bed.

Fake dating your ex to save Christmas...
what could go wrong?

For the reader who said, and I quote, "but do we have to wait until 54% for him to lick her nipple?"

In this book, you do not!

Canadian Glossary

This book is set in Canada, so it uses Canadian English spelling and vocabulary! There are also some medical training details that are specific to this region of the world, too. If you have any questions about what you think might be a "Canadian-ism", join the Pine Harbour Spicy Book Club on Facebook!

toque: a knit winter hat (also called a beanie); this is pronounced like the number two with a hard k on the end; two-k

ice wine: a sweet dessert wine made from grapes that freeze on the vine; it's not exclusively Canadian (it originated in Germany), but Canada is now the leading producer of it because our climate is well suited to it, and it's very popular here

Boxing Day: a stat holiday, the day after Christmas

stat holiday: what Canadians call a regulated day off, like a federal holiday or bank holiday, but they vary by province!

PGY5: post graduate year five, this refers to the year of residency training a doctor is in. In Canada, OB/GYN trainees do five years of residency. (This is different from the United States, where they do four years of training)

Chapter 1

Rory

August

What are you going to do, send your ex a booty call?

No. Of course not.

He wouldn't be up for that even if I did.

Every muscle in my body aches from fatigue and barely restrained frustration. So there's no good reason why I'm staring at Garrett's text messages at eleven o'clock at night.

Since we broke up in April, we've exchanged five messages. All breakup related, all very polite.

But before that...

I scroll back.

Before that was an endless stream of late night messages. Me texting him that I was on my way home from the hospital. Him sending back an encouraging emoji or a funny meme. A promise of something good on the stove for a late dinner. An offer of a foot rub or a hot shower.

He always took good care of me, and I...

I put my phone down and blow a raspberry at the

ceiling of our too-quiet condo. *Not our condo anymore.* Just mine, now.

For ten more months, anyway. Then I'll...

Well, I'm not sure where I'm going at the end of this year of residency training. *Fuck.*

I shove off the couch and force myself to go take a hot shower. The water feels good on my back, my shoulders... my tits.

I grab the wand off the hook and think about trying to use it to get off. I tease the spray over my nipples, then lower, over my belly to the juncture of my legs.

But it's not easy for me to come like this, and the shower has too many memories of Garrett anyway.

I take my birth control pill, then brush my teeth.

The pill package glares at me from the shelf. It's not like I have a pressing reason to keep taking them, other than I have every night since I was seventeen and Garrett and I started having sex.

And the quiet panic that if I stop a routine, I might never get back into it.

I don't pick up habits easily. Completing twelve years of post-secondary school and taking birth control pills for that entire time is really the only consistent thing I've been successful at.

Ironic that my tunnel vision is the reason I don't need the pills anymore. There are other ways I could manage my heavy periods. I blow a raspberry and adjust the packet on the shelf.

Stop thinking about Garrett.

My thumb taps against the perforation I just made in the foil. Smack in the middle of my cycle.

Oh, for fuck's sake. I'm ovulating.

I laugh out loud. Okay. I just need to rub one out in bed and then crash, and I'll feel better in the morning.

As I check that my alarms are set for the morning, I consider texting Garrett. Would he chuckle?

Have we reached that stage in our breakup where we can laugh at the past?

RORY

You're probably asleep, but I just realized something funny

GARRETT

Not asleep

Oh. That was fast.

RORY

You know how you always knew when I was ovulating?

He doesn't reply to that.
Shit.

RORY

The punchline is that I realized in the shower that the combination of a bad day at work + unexpectedly persistent thoughts about you probably has a hormonal trigger

Never mind, it was funnier in my head

Dots appear. Disappear. And then after a long, agonizing pause, a message pops onto the screen.

GARRETT

You saying you're horny, Roar?

RORY

Sorry, I know that's not okay

I'm just lonely, I want to add, but I can't tell him that. Him being my entire social life is part of why we broke up.

GARRETT

Get yourself off and you'll fall asleep in
no time

I stare at the words, hating how well he knows me.

RORY

I know

GARRETT

Did you try?

Is there any way to answer that without crossing a line?

RORY

Yeah, in the shower

GARRETT

With the shower head?

That doesn't work for you

RORY

Desperate times call for desperate
measures

GARRETT

Are you in bed now?

RORY

Mmhmm

GARRETT

Use your fingers

RORY

We shouldn't be doing this

GARRETT

What are we doing?

RORY

I don't know

GARRETT

I'm at a bar right now, so if you're worried about me being a perv with your texts, you're safe

RORY

If anything, I'm the perv right now

GARRETT

Why?

I can't tell him. I press my thighs tight together, clamping down on my hand, trying to contain my aching need.

GARRETT

You touching yourself right now?

RORY

Yes

GARRETT

Is it enough?

RORY

No

GARRETT

Have you changed the door code?

I jerk upright in bed. He's not offering...is he?
Oh my God, he is.
Heat blazes through me. My breasts are instantly heavy, my thighs tense. This is a terrible idea, of course, but...

RORY

Still the same

GARRETT

Be right there

"Noooo..." I breathe.

But my racing pulse says otherwise.

I scramble out of bed, looking at my laundry piles. The basket that needs to be washed on my day off. The basket I washed on my last day off and never put away. The chair that holds all the in between things that can be worn again, probably, before needing to be—

"He doesn't care about laundry," I mutter.

This is a booty call, right? I change into a lacy tank top and panties set, then feel ridiculous, so I pull my comfy sleep clothes back on over top.

I might faint.

I make the bed, ignoring the panicky weird feelings about how it's where we used to have sex, and how it might feel to have him tumble back into this space with me. Then I run back to the bathroom. There's no time to shave anything, but maybe a quick trim of the pubes? Is that desperate? He didn't care about that while we were together, but what if he has new standards now?

He was so fast to offer the hookup. Is he the hookup king now?

My stomach flip-flops at that thought. *Hate* that, actually. And I know pills won't be enough. I dig in my backpack, hoping that I have some condoms from the last sexual health workshop I gave—*yes, thank you past Rory, for being a pack rat*—and then there's no more time to think about if this is a good idea or not because I can hear his footsteps on the stairs.

The knock is quiet, a slow double tap of his knuckles on a door he once lived behind.

He looks good. As tall as ever, but he looks bigger. Broader. He fills the doorway. It's been a couple of months since I last saw him. How much muscle can a lean, lanky guy pack on over a single summer? He's wearing a plaid flannel shirt over a faded green t-shirt from the garage he works at, the colour making his pale blue-green eyes brighter than I remember. Every little detail gets catalogued. His black jeans are old, but he's wearing boots I've never seen before. His golden brown hair has gotten long, compared to how he used to wear it, and it's starting to curl.

It's all painfully familiar, but new and unfamiliar in specific ways at the same time.

"That was fast." There's an edge of suspicion in my voice. Not a great start to whatever this is we're about to do.

He ignores it and rakes his gaze over my long-sleeve t-shirt and cotton sleep shorts. The way his attention sharpens when he gets to my bare legs makes my stomach take flight. "I was just down the street."

I dig the hole a little deeper. "On a date?"

"You think I'd ditch a date to respond to your orgasm distress signal?" Does he look...amused?

"I'm not *distressed*."

He just stares at me. No, not amused.

Heat crawls up my neck. "Is that what you got from my messages? This was a mistake. Nice to see you, Garrett. You look really good. I'm sorry that I texted you, but—"

He cuts me off. "You gotta be up in the morning, right? I'll tuck you in."

It feels like I'm in free fall. "I don't know—"

He snaps his hand forward, catching the hem of my shirt, hooking his index finger under it and using that to tug me closer to him. "You do, Roar. You texted me because your brain is racing and you need to sleep, and I know how to make that happen for you. I wouldn't be here if I didn't want to get my mouth on your sweet little stressed-out pussy, okay? So shut up and let me help."

I shudder, months of loneliness and repressed desire surging back into painful awareness. *Help.* Will it still feel like helping in the morning?

But then again, in the morning, I'll be run off my feet with rounds and consults. In the morning, it won't matter that I'm lonely. I'll be too busy to be lonely.

Just like I was too busy for Garrett when he was mine.

"I'd owe you one," I joke. "That could get complicated."

He doesn't laugh.

He just spins me around and presses me against the door. And somehow, he manages not to touch any bare skin until he brushes his fingertips against my wrist.

"You're wearing a lot of clothes for a girl who wants to come," he whispers, his breath warm against the back of my neck. "I'm going to take them off you."

I shiver and nod as he tugs my sleeve off. I help despite the alarm bells going off in my head, pulling my arms in, and then he slides it over my head.

He groans when he sees I'm wearing a lacy tank top underneath it, and I shouldn't feel a rush of something like pride at having an effect on him, but there it is anyway. A wild, roiling sensation that leaves me feeling reckless.

I twist my head to the side, thinking I might kiss him, but his hand slides into my hair, stopping me. He gently presses my cheek back to the door.

"Hold still for me," he urges. "Just...feel."

His other hand trails over my shoulder and down my

arm, catching my wrist, tugging it above my head and stretching me onto my tiptoes.

"Okay?"

I nod. Yeah. More than okay. The noise in my head fades to a muzzy static, and he slides his touch down my arm again, down my front this time, into my tank top.

"Fuck," he whispers when he cups my breast.

I know. I can feel it, too. My nipple is so hard against his palm, straining against his touch.

My thighs shake as I hold myself up on my toes.

Time freezes for a charged, confusing beat. Garrett breathing against the back of my neck, curving over me. My head spinning as he just holds my tit and makes me stay in that stretched up position.

Waiting and wanting.

And then, with a growl, he pulls off my tank top before pressing his hips in against me. I can feel his erection, thick and hard against my butt, and as he cups my bared breasts in his hands, his face falls to the curve of my neck.

It's a relief knowing he's turned on, too. But that pulse of awareness is followed immediately by another bolt of irritation, that this is so easy for him.

"You're so fucking hot." He drags in a breath, then slides one hand down my bare belly, his fingertips pushing along the waistband of my sleep shorts. "Let's get you to bed."

"I don't need to be tucked in." The words rush out of me, getting tighter as my throat feels like it's going to close up.

I can't handle him in the bed we once shared.

He pushes his hand just into my panties. Still teasing. Unaffected by my flutter of panic. "Couch, then?"

"Here's just fine by me." I push my ass back against his erection. "Make it quick against the door?"

He huffs a laugh against my temple. "That eager to kick me out?"

"Just trying to keep it simple."

"I'll leave my boots on, then. Any other demands? Lights on or off?"

We've always been lights on people, so I'm guessing he's asking if I want to pretend this is more anonymous or something.

"On," I pant.

If he's gotten jacked over the summer, I want to see it.

I didn't know that the last time we ever had sex would be the last time. I can't even remember exactly when it was.

This time? I'm going to catalogue every single second.

With a nod, he pushes my shorts down, then steps back.

In the sudden absence of his body, I sway, dropping back to my heels. By the time I turn around, he's peeled off his flannel shirt and stretched out on my new sofa, his feet hanging just over the end. I should hate that he's left his boots on, but it helps anchor what this is—and what this isn't. And they're not touching the couch.

Enough thinking about the sofa, I scold myself.

I'm naked.

He's laying down.

I look at where his erection is straining against the fly of his jeans.

"I've got condoms," I say.

It sounds inane out loud. So matter of fact. Is this what casual sex feels like? I wouldn't know. He's the only person I've ever done this with.

His eyes rake over me, making my skin pebble. "We

don't need them for you to ride my face. Get your ass over here."

Heat races to my cheeks, and my legs shake as I cross to him. "I'm just saying I think we need to be sensible—"

He catches me by the hips as soon as I'm within grabbing range and he pulls me on top of him, so I'm straddling his chest. "You think too fucking much."

And then he latches his mouth onto a nipple and sucks.

Fuck.

White hot need pulses straight through me, arrowing directly to my pussy. I breathe his name.

He pulls off with a wet pop, then drags his nose along my skin, inhaling before he takes the other nipple between his teeth and licks it.

I've missed this so much.

Shame twists around my pulsing desire. We really shouldn't be doing this.

I shouldn't let him tug my hips up, shouldn't moan as he bites at my belly and kisses my inner thighs while he positions them on either side of his head.

I shouldn't brace my hands on the arm of the sofa and hold myself up so he can spread me open and look at me, his gaze burning dark and rabid.

All those *shouldn'ts* make me hesitate, and he notices.

"What, you think I've lost my taste for this? Sit on my fucking face, Roar."

A whole body shiver rockets through me as he wraps his long arms around my thighs, taking full control.

Locking me in for the ride.

A decade of memories slam through me as he licks a broad path straight up my centre to my clit.

When was the first time we did it like this?

God, it's hard to remember when his tongue is doing *that*.

Was it the first winter here in Ottawa? I moved for university, and I was living in the dorms, but I hated my roommate. Garrett was visiting, and he went to the military recruiting office.

Would I want to move off-campus and share an apartment, if he could get into a reserve unit in Ottawa?

I threw myself at him, and after making out hungrily, he asked me to sit on his face.

"But...how will you breathe?"

He just grinned and shrugged. "Dunno."

"Garrett!" My face was burning up. "If I smother you..."

"Then I'll die the happiest recruit in the Canadian Forces."

He didn't die. It sort of felt like *I* did, the best kind of death, the type of orgasm that builds and builds with heady need, pulse-pounding and intense, and then explodes into dazzling nothingness.

That same kind of release is starting to coil tight in my belly now, as he pulls my clit into his mouth, as he licks and sucks and *growls*.

Missed you, I want to say. But I don't, because that isn't what this is. He won't even let me kiss him. He picked the crudest way to get me off.

This is just sex.

That splashes cold water on my arousal.

My hips stutter, my thighs tensing up, as suddenly his mouth on my clit is too much, way too much.

"Garrett, stop," I pant.

He pulls off gasping.

How will you breathe?

Dunno.

He stares up at me, his face slick with my arousal.

"It's okay," he says. "You taste good. Don't over think it."

I let out a weak little laugh. "Easier said than done."

He rolls his eyes. "Jesus Christ."

I frown. "Hey, I can't *help* it."

He pats my hip. "Lift up."

I pull my shaking leg off him, and he slides out from under me. He doesn't go far, just circles around and holds me from behind. My ass rubs against his erection as he hooks my bare legs around his kneeling thighs.

Stretching me out, a naked girl on top of her fully-clothed ex.

"Look at how fucking sexy you are," he whispers roughly in my ear. He palms my tits, then pushes one hand between my thighs. His fingers tease at my pussy lips, but he avoids my clit. "You were all turned on when we started. Was it the bickering that did it for you? You sent out an orgasm distress signal, but you really just wanted to fight?"

I choke on a frustrated denial.

"Yeah, no. You want to come." He works his middle finger through my slick arousal to my entrance. "So stop thinking and fuck my hand."

I roll my hips, grinding back against his thick cock. "Your hand isn't why I texted you."

He keeps going as if I didn't just beg for his dick. "Jesus, fighting makes you wet."

"I have condoms, so it's fine if you've been—"

He pinches my clit. "Let's go find you a toy."

"Okay, you can go home now." I wriggle out of his arms and stumble off the couch. His green flannel shirt is the closest thing I can find to cover my naked body.

"Whoa, hang on." He frowns as he climbs to his feet.

He's so much taller than me.

When we were together, he was such a constant in my life that he never felt tall to me, he was just *Garrett*.

But with a few months' absence, he's now a stranger. A more muscular, taller, more *frustrating* stranger.

And despite my hot and cold attitude, he still has a very prominent erection. Plus he's breathing so hard, his whole chest is rising and falling.

"You always do this!" I yell. "You think you can control the conversation by just avoiding what I'm saying, and that's—"

"And you always self-sabotage a good thing," he says quietly, cutting me off. Firm and unrepentant.

The direct shot takes my breath away.

God damn it. Hot tears threaten behind my eyelids. "I need to go to bed."

"Don't fucking—" He exhales roughly. "I got my dick pierced."

"What?"

"That's why I was dodging what you were saying. I thought I could just get you off and we wouldn't have to talk about it." His cheeks slash with ruddy embarrassment.

"You..." I drop my eyes and stare at his bulge. "Why?"

He doesn't answer.

I tighten my hold on his shirt.

I shared a bed—a whole life—with Garrett for a decade, and I never had a glimmer of a guess that he would want to get *pierced*.

One summer apart, and he's changed more than I could imagine.

"Did you think I would judge you for it?" I huff a definitely-not-jealous laugh. "Have you had any bad reactions?"

"Are we asking each other about our personal lives now?" He reaches out and tugs on the shirt I've wrapped around myself. "I got them done for myself. That's all you need to know."

"Them? There's more than one?"

He unbuttons his jeans. The metallic purr of his zipper is so loud, I realize I'm holding my breath.

His fingers hesitate at the waistband of his black boxer briefs, then he frees his cock. Even with his fingers holding up the heavy length, I can see a Jacob's Ladder down the underside of his cock. Three prominent barbells.

My eyes bug out.

"You sure you want to get on this ride again? There's been some modifications."

"Don't underestimate the power of curiosity," I mutter as I yank off his shirt and let it drop to the floor in front of him. I follow, licking my lips as I get on my knees, then take him in my mouth.

God, they feel wild on my tongue. I swallow him as deep as I can go, then slide off. He makes the most incredible sound as I lick the barbells out of my mouth, then swirl that eager spit around his tip.

He catches my head in his hands and holds me still.

His cock is wet in my hand, wet from my mouth, and my lips feel swollen already.

I can't read his expression. But when he growls low in his throat and thrusts his hips forward, that's clear as can be. I swallow him again and moan around his length.

He fucks my mouth, using my tongue, using his new decorations. It's a wicked combination. He gets bigger than I remember, until he's heavy on my tongue and my mouth is stretched wide.

With a gasp, he wrenches out of me and pushes me onto all fours.

"Where are those fucking condoms?" His voice is

ragged but his touch is firm, confident as he mounts me from behind.

I can't see him, but I can feel the shiver-inducing heavy weight of his cock, bumping against my ass, and the rip of a wrapper completes the picture of what he's doing.

I stretch my arms out in front of me and lower my head, letting my hips rise to meet him. Letting go of everything else. All thought, any worry.

Nothing else matters but receiving the thick press of Garrett's cock. Of being fucked and enjoying it for what it is. A gift, pure pleasure.

And it's so good once I let everything else go. He stretches me on the way in, and I'm not even sure I feel the piercings as he buries himself to the hilt, but I for sure feel them as he rocks his hips back.

I feel the heck out of them in the best way.

"Holy shit," I breathe.

He tightens his hold on my hips. "Yeah? Good?"

"Harder."

He snaps forward, driving deep.

"Yes," I pant. "More."

He shifts his thighs wider, adding the weight of his body to the next soul-thudding thrust. It's perfect.

Cursing, he curves over me, covering my back with his body. His t-shirt clings to the damp sweat on my back. He presses his forehead to my shoulder and picks up the pace. One of his hands wraps around to find my clit.

That extra pressure is all I need to shoot off like a rocket.

It's not the kind of orgasm I was chasing when I was on his face. It's not the kind of orgasm I was thinking about at all. It's the kind of bright, short bursting climax I needed, something...functional. It floods my body with the hormones I was craving, and I go boneless, sagging to the floor as Garret fucks me harder, chasing his own release.

"Give me another, Roar," he growls against my hair.

I can't, I want to say, but the words don't come out. And then it turns out I can, it turns out that his clever mechanic fingers know exactly how to play my clit, even after a long break.

And as he circles my still-throbbing nerve centre, I feel a deeper orgasm gathering like storm clouds, heavy and dark. Racing in on a rush of hot, late summer wind.

"Fucking come for me," he grunts. "Need you to—"

I sob his name, jerking my hips up to meet his long, deep, desperate final thrusts.

He loses control, rolling up and hard into me in a way that drives his piercings over a new spot inside, and I see an entire galaxy of stars.

"Fuck, yes," he gasps. "I can feel you. That's it. Squeeze me. Milk me. God damn."

And then there's stillness.

Neither of us move. We barely breathe. Deep inside me, he pulses, and have I ever felt that before? Has he ever taken up this much space inside me before?

"Shit," he mutters.

Then, "Sorry."

"For what? The double orgasm or the rug burn on my knees? I think I needed all of that."

He pushes off me, taking that delicious fullness with him, leaving me feeling wrung out and empty in a good way. In a *I'm going to sleep well* kind of way.

"I probably shouldn't sleep right here on the floor," I mumble.

"I'll get you a glass of water."

"I'm fine."

"You get dehydrated."

"I can take care of myself." I hear myself as I say it. And I know he's holding his tongue when he doesn't immediately snap back that he's only here since I was whining that I can't.

He covers me with something soft, then lets himself out.

I drift in the warm, muzzy post-orgasm glow until the middle of the night.

Then I stumble to the kitchen to drink water I should have let him get me before rolling myself into bed.

It's not until I get up in the morning that I realize he left his flannel shirt behind. That's what he covered me with. It smells like us, like sex and desperation.

I toss it in the to-wash laundry basket and race to the shower, where I promise myself out loud that I'll figure out how to use the damn shower head to get off.

Because last night?

That can't happen again.

Chapter 2

Garrett

September

"Don't even pretend you didn't want this," I warn Rory as she trembles through an orgasm aftershock.

"We all want things that are bad for us," she pants back. And then, maybe because she's still shaking, she adds, "Or things that are too good."

Since she didn't text me again after our first hookup, it couldn't have been *that* good. Not until she was ovulating again.

I know how to count. I can picture the mini pills she takes to keep her periods manageable—and I try not to think about the fact that she wants us to use condoms now, too, even though her nightly pill was always enough in the past.

It's none of my business what she does with anyone else. I'll focus on the fact they aren't who she turns to at her horniest time of the month.

This time, I made sure to get her off with my mouth before I yanked her down my body and shoved my cock in her tight, wet heat.

We also managed to stay on the couch, but that's where the civility ended.

"I think I scratched you," Rory mumbles into my neck.

"You offering to do first aid?"

Her lips move against my skin, but she doesn't reply. Just exhales as she pats my shoulder, then climbs off my lap.

Yeah, it's time for me to go. I've been here for an hour, and I can feel the walls closing in.

In the months leading to our breakup, I started to notice that we could spend about ninety minutes together before tension would boil over. After a decade of never fighting, an hour and a half fuse was suffocating.

Now it's an irritatingly short window to cram as much hot, desperate sex into as I can manage, so she'll hopefully slide into my messages again.

She picks her panties up from the floor and hops into them. Then she crosses her arms over her bare tits and glares at me. "Do you have plans tomorrow morning?"

My whole body tightens up. I'm not sure I heard her correctly. "You want to get breakfast?"

She snorts as if that's ridiculous. "I want you to meet me at the hospital after morning rounds so I can suck your cock again."

Ah. Just sex. "Sure, I'm free. Whenever you want."

She frowns. "This shouldn't become a routine for us."

"Because orgasms are terrible."

"Because we broke up."

"Don't worry, I haven't forgotten." But there's a huge difference between *shouldn't* and *won't*. After two incredibly hot hookups, and her already wanting a repeat in the morning, I'm pretty confident that I'll be getting another text from Rory before too long.

Whether that's healthy, though.... That's another question.

She's clearly thinking the same thoughts. "I'm just saying, we need to fully get it out of our systems. Completely. So there's no more...."

I raise my eyebrows. "No more what?"

"Never mind." Right on schedule, Rory shuts down, like spending time with me is exhausting. And maybe it is. Maybe I asked too much of her when we were together.

Lesson learned.

If she just wants a hookup, that's all I'll be for her.

Of course I make myself available the next morning. She's waiting outside the hospital when I pull up, and after hopping in, she directs me to a parking lot not far from the hospital.

"I got you a breakfast sandwich," I say as I pull away from the curb. "And coffee."

"That wasn't necessary."

She grabs it, though, doesn't she? "Better than a vending machine."

"No commentary required."

"Name one hot meal you've had this week."

"We're not doing this."

"Doing what? Talking about basic self-care?" I hold up my hand, cutting off her protest. "Fine. The only help I'm allowed to offer is orgasmic. Got it."

"Garrett—"

I pull into the thankfully empty parking lot. We might

not even have ninety minutes this morning, so I better make what time we do have count.

She takes one last bite of her sandwich, then shoves it in the brown paper bag as I undo her seatbelt.

I fucking love scrubs. They're so easy to slide my hand into.

I get her off first, my lips against her ear alternating between dirty talk and reminders that we could get caught —which, for Rory this morning, counts as dirty talk, too.

"Don't close your eyes. If you close your eyes, who's going to tell me to stop if someone pulls in next to us?"

All she has for that is a weak moan, because I've got my fingers on her pulsing clit and I can feel how close she is.

"Why'd you pick this spot?" I nip at her ear when she doesn't reply. "Want to get caught?"

"N-no." And then she shudders, her thighs clamping tight around my hand, coating my fingers with a flood of arousal.

"Fucking beautiful," I growl.

As soon as she releases her python grip on my hand, I lift my fingers to my mouth, licking them clean.

She blushes, and that makes her taste all the sweeter. I didn't appreciate her blushes enough when we were together.

"My turn," she says breathlessly.

Fuck, I shouldn't like how eager she is to get her tongue on my piercings again. But then she does, and her fingers too, and thinking is beyond me. I explode in her mouth with embarrassing speed, but she seems pleased that she was able to pull that from me so quickly.

She doesn't notice me staring at her lips as she chugs the lukewarm coffee, then fixes her scrubs.

Her pager goes off as I pull up to the hospital.

"Thanks," she tosses over her shoulder as she reads the message.

"Did that get it fully out of your system this time?"

She stops reading.

Thin ice, bud. I keep going, though. "Yeah, me neither. See you next month."

"Bold assumption," she mutters.

Ah. So she's still not comfortable with whatever it is we're doing here. Fair enough. I shrug. "Sure. You're the one with the busy schedule."

I don't bother to point out she's also the one with the hormonal cravings.

Chapter 3

Rory

October

I need to return Garrett's flannel shirt, that's all. There's no other reason for me to text him this month.

It's not because I wake up in the middle of the night, my sheets twisted around my legs, as if I'm burning up because it's been twenty-eight days since I've had his dick in my body.

That can't be it.

"You look tired," the junior OB/GYN resident says as I join her in front of the whiteboard in Labour & Delivery.

A headache threatens as I skim the cases we have admitted for now, and the expected elective surgeries on the schedule. "And you look like you still have three and a half years of residency ahead of you, and have no idea what's around the corner, so mind your own beeswax."

Undeterred, she follows me into the break room. "Are you scrubbing in on the c-sections this morning?"

"Yep, and so are you."

"Can I—"

"No." I pour myself a coffee.

"You didn't even let me finish!"

"Whatever it is, the answer is no." I gesture for her to keep following me. "You're not in a position to ask for things yet. Go where people tell you to go."

"What about taking initiative?"

I set my coffee down, shove some charts into her arms. "Here's your initiative. Find two cases in here that you aren't familiar with and have questions about for rounds."

And then I grab my coffee, dig out my phone, and hide in an empty patient room to fire Garrett a quick message.

RORY

Hey, so I still have your green flannel shirt

GARRETT

Have you been wearing it to bed for the last two months?

You wish

I prefer to think of you sleeping naked

We aren't flirting

That's for later, then?

Don't you think the long stretches of time in which you don't hear from me would be a clear message that I'm not trying to get something going again?

Don't worry, Roar, I know that we aren't getting back together

You broke up with me

And we don't need to rehash why that
happened when there are more urgent
things to talk about, like the fact your
pussy can't spontaneously combust
without the right accelerant

He attaches a photo, but it doesn't load because the
signal sucks in this part of the hospital.

RORY

Do not send me a dick pic at work!

GARRETT

You're the one pre-booking me for a booty
call later like I'm an airport town car hire

It's not a dick pic

It's worse. It's a selfie, taken in the garage. It looks like
he's flexing, like he knows that the forearm porn is even
better than a dick pic.

I can't fall for that propaganda.

RORY

You know what? I'll just mail you the shirt

GARRETT

Keep it, the days are getting colder

I shove my phone in my pocket and head to rounds.

The rest of the day is slammed, and I'm run off my
feet. We have two straightforward surgeries and one with
some complications because it's the patient's fifth section,
which should be a great teaching opportunity. But the
consultant on call wants to get through it quickly, which
makes it shitty for the junior residents who have scrubbed
in.

And then as we're scrubbing out, *I'm* the one the junior resident takes it out on.

"You could have advocated for us!" Her voice cracks. "We're here to learn."

"Stick around and you'll probably get to scrub in for some emergency sections overnight."

"I can't."

I slide her a sideways glance. "You *can't*?"

"I have a kid. A family. It's not unreasonable to hope to get my teachable moments during schedule surgeries."

I open my mouth to tell her she needs to toughen up, that I went through the same thing and—

The words die in my throat.

Because I didn't go through the same thing, did I?

I don't have a kid. I don't have a family waiting for me at home. I don't even have Garrett anymore, because I made my life so razor-thin, so narrow-focused on work, that there wasn't room for him in it anymore. Not the way he wanted.

But before all of that...

I remember wanting to get out of here at night. Wanting to race home to my boyfriend's arms, to dinner and a snuggle on the couch.

So in a way, I can see myself in her frustrated tears. Four years ago, standing in this exact spot, fighting to get meaningful cases from my senior resident. And what did he tell me?

Suck it up, buttercup. This is how we've always done it.

I sucked it up better than anyone. I got harder. I stopped expecting teaching moments. I learned to grab lessons where I could, stealing glimpses of technique between the insults and exhaustion. And I rose to be chief resident, only to turn around and repeat the cycle.

"I'm sorry," I say, and her anger deflates into confusion.

"You're right to feel like you missed out. I could have advocated for you more in that moment."

She blinks at me, suspicious. "Really?"

I lean against the scrub sink, suddenly feeling every one of my thirty years. "Tomorrow, I'll bring this up with whoever is in the OR. I'll explain that you missed out today. I promise. And we can grab lunch and talk about the cases."

The junior resident stares at me in disbelief, then mutters a super-fast thank you and bolts before I can change my mind.

I check my phone. Garrett still hasn't texted again.

I have a bunch of other text chains that I'm derelict on, though. A dusty group chat with my sisters. Jules, aka Baby Minelli, got a new job in the summer that she's wildly excited about, nannying for a divorced power couple. He's a professional athlete and she's a...singer? Actress? I can't remember what she told us before signing an NDA that she takes super seriously. Which leaves Cassie—the only one of us to stay in Pine Harbour—to send a weekly check-in message.

Wincing, I drop a heart on her most recent one. Proof of life.

I also owe a reply to my Aunt Mara, my mom's youngest sister. The day I started as chief resident, she sent me a text message that cut a little too close to the truth.

MARA

I know this year is going to be the hardest yet for you, my ferocious niece! Stay strong.

And then she included a sketch of me as a fearsome monster.

Since then, she's sent me variations on the same sketch.

Never asking me how I'm doing, as if she knows from a distance that the answer is *not great*. Just gifting me a little bit of inspirational joy every few weeks.

I either reply immediately or never, there is no in between.

But I want to be better. I look at the most recent drawing, which I saw in between surgeries a few days ago. My heart squeezes.

RORY

I love these messages, btw. I know I don't reply often.

Dots appear as soon as I hit send.

MARA

I know you're busy.

RORY

I don't want to be too busy for my family.

MARA

You won't always be. This is a season in your life, that's all.

RORY

I feel selfish.

MARA

Oh, sweetness. Don't worry about that. Sometimes we need to be selfish in this world to get what we want.

RORY

Ahhh it's so hard to remember that and not feel guilty

MARA

Will I see you at Christmas?

RORY

> Absolutely, I already have that week
> blocked off

MARA

> I'll be sure to remind you then

An alarm goes off on my phone. A reminder to myself to eat dinner. Shit. I race to the cafeteria, thinking about what my aunt said the whole way.

She was talking about work. I agree with her that it's good for girls—women—to be selfish and protect their dreams.

But when I told her I feel selfish, I mean it in more ways than just that.

Since I can't very well ask her about how to manage whatever this is I'm doing with Garrett, that only leaves me one person to consult on the question pinging around in my brain.

On a scale of one to incredibly selfish, how terrible am I being using you for sex?

Can I ask him that?

Fuck it.

I type it out and hit send.

GARRETT

> You aren't terrible

RORY

> It's messed up, though

GARRETT

> Are you looking for a fight?

RORY

> No

GARRETT

What time are you going to get home
tonight?

My stomach flip flops at the directness. At the promise of something other than a fight, but...still close to a fight. Still not right.

I want it so much. Too much. I want it enough that my hands shake as I type out a message turning it down, because I should, even though I really don't want to.

RORY

I'm working all night, unfortunately...our junior resident can't sleep here so I'm in the call room

GARRETT

Okay

That's it. Easy acceptance. As far as closure goes, it's pretty weak, but it'll have to do. That has to be the last text messages we exchange. I need to re-focus on what really matters, and I can't be selfish in every quadrant of my life.

Chapter 4

Garrett

November

Well, fuck.

Chapter 5

Rory

December

Happy holidays

Hey stranger

I still have that shirt of yours

I should get that from you...are you
heading home for Christmas?

Are you?

Don't sound so surprised

Were you thinking of something sooner?

Tonight, maybe?

Did I lose you

No

Yeah, maybe tonight

> I'm going to need you to use your words

> I was hoping you might be free tonight, yes

> For sex

> Is that enough words?

> I'll be there in fifteen

> Wear the shirt

"Bossy," I mutter.

But I wear the shirt.

It's warm and cozy in the condo, but cold outside. The first blast of winter hit Quebec and eastern Ontario today, and when Garrett arrives, he's wearing a heavy parka over jeans and boots.

Snow dusts the tips of his golden brown hair, and his cheeks are pink slashes above a close-cropped beard that's new.

He always felt too big for this small condo, especially in those last few months as our relationship fell apart. The little break again since the end of the summer has only exacerbated the effect. Now his larger-than-life presence—big, broad, and painfully tense—fills the air around me, making it hard to breathe.

"You rang for service?"

"Don't say it like that."

He tugs off his gloves and goes to put them on the side table that used to be beside the door, but I sold it last week.

After staring at the empty spot for a second, Garrett lets the gloves fall to the floor with a wet thunk.

Then he unzips his jacket.

Tonight he's wearing a dark grey ribbed Henley that clings to his broad chest.

I want to cling to his chest, too.

He hangs up his coat (on the hooks he installed when we moved into this place four-and-a-half years ago) and then gestures at his feet. The unspoken question is, *do you even want me to take off my boots?*

"Oh for fuck's sake," I burst out. I don't need this performance. If he's changed his mind, he can just go. We're already broken up, he can just jog back down to his truck and head on out of my life, never for our paths to cross again.

I go to open the door, to shove him out to the hallway, but as soon as I'm within arm's reach, he scoops me up. All the air whooshes out of my lungs and I make a little sound, *unfff*, that barely escapes before his thumb brushes across my lips.

As if to remind me we get along better when we don't talk.

Because when we talk, we fight. But we don't fight when he closes the gap between us and drags his nose along my jaw, then the tip of his tongue along the outside curve of my ear.

No, we've never had a problem with instant chemistry.

My arms go around his neck, my fingers pushing up into his hair—it's getting longer each month, like he hasn't bothered to cut it even once since we broke up—and under his shirt, needing to touch his back.

His lips are cold but the rest of him is hot. Hot muscles flexing beneath my fingertips. Hot mouth sucking on that spot halfway down my neck that makes my knees weak.

It isn't fair, how well he knows my body. How easily he gets my blood pumping.

"Stop fucking thinking," he growls.

If only. That's why he's here, though. He knows how to push me into that blissfully quiet space.

"What do you need?"

That's a more Garrett thing to ask. Less sharp than *you rang for service?*

But both are on point. I need him, because his mouth chases my worries away, if only for an hour.

One of his hands curves down to the hem of his shirt and then his fingers are gripping my bare ass, shoving under the elastic of my panties. Electricity streaks across my skin, leaving goosebumps in its wake.

We really shouldn't be doing this, and that makes this even hotter.

You are a doctor, Rory Minelli. This is shameful behaviour.

But I don't care. I tried to make our relationship work, and when it ended, I tried to move on. Doing the right thing in both spaces had failed miserably.

Maybe once I finish my residency, I can spend some time figuring out why only Garrett works me up like this. For now, in the few spare hours I have, I don't want—

"Jesus Christ," he growls. "You're fucking soaked for me."

His fingers have unerringly found the seam of my sex and now he's stroking my pussy lips, making my slickness spill free.

I moan.

"Call me up so I can come over and be witness to how messy you are on the inside." His voice sounds like it is underneath my skin now, rough and raw. "When did you start to ache today, Rory? Was it all day?"

I shake my head. Not quite all day. But by lunch, my

thoughts were on him. On his voice and his hands and his cock.

And I can't deny it, because he made me use my words when I texted him.

An advantage of fucking your ex is that there is no confusion about what one wants. I wouldn't text him if I weren't horny. He wouldn't have messaged back if he didn't feel the same way.

We don't need to pretend that we aren't desperate for this.

That he doesn't want to get his fingers inside my pussy. That I'm not aching to unzip his fly and get my hands on—

As if he can read my mind, he grabs my wrist and pulls my hand up over my head.

His mouth drags along my jaw, and my heart freezes for a second, wondering if he'll kiss me this time.

We haven't yet.

Not since two days before we broke up in April.

I've gone nine months without kissing him.

Now I'm thinking about his mouth, how good his tongue would feel against mine, and that's the opposite of where my head should be at. We should be de-escalating this.

And yet I yearn for his mouth.

"Garrett," I whine, twisting my face, seeking him out.

He releases my pinned wrist and pushes those fingers over my tongue instead. I wrap my arm around his neck and give in, letting him fuck my pussy and my mouth with his hands. Letting him invade my body and chase away my thoughts about how to tell our parents we aren't together anymore. Christmas is right around the corner.

"Jesus, your mouth is so fucking hungry, isn't it?" He

pulls his hands off me long enough to suck his fingers, then he's unbuckling his belt. "Get on your knees."

He yanks off his shirt and leans his bare back against the door.

"You've been working out," I say.

"Rugby."

"Rugby?"

He fists his cock and taps it against my mouth. "This isn't going to suck itself."

Rugby?

Garrett has always been fit. He works with his hands all day as a mechanic and has to maintain a certain standard for his military reserve responsibilities. But he's never been athletic, per se.

This new rugby-built body is impressive. He looked jacked in the summer, and now he's...solid. Super solid.

I feast my eyes on his firm muscles and the fine line of blond hair running down his belly, to the golden brown curls at the base of his cock. And then to the silver balls peeking out between his curved fingers.

"Sorry," I whisper against the head of his cock, my lips brushing his exposed crown as he slides the foreskin back. "I was distracted by how obnoxiously good you look."

He grunts and presses my bottom lip down, making me show him my tongue.

It's all so rough and vaguely degrading and completely perfect.

When he pushes in, it's easy, because my mouth is watering for the thick stretch. Those piercings still feel wild against my tongue, a few months haven't softened the reaction there. And the power I have, even on my knees, to make him come apart so quickly, is *amazing*.

It makes me feel like I could fly, like I could do anything I want. So strange. So fun.

I swallow him right to the root, until it's hard to breathe and think and do anything but find a rhythm that allows me to do that again and again.

He swells against my tongue, his skin stretching taught, his seed pulsing onto the roof of my mouth and down my throat. His scent gets into my brain and makes me moan as I suck him faster and faster.

"You're gonna make me come. Stop. God, that's too good. That's so..." He grips my hair and tugs me off, glaring down at me in a way that makes me laugh.

"Don't you want to?" I lick my lips. "It's all I've been thinking about all day."

His chest heaves. "Not this fast. You come first." He hauls me to my feet. "Preferably twice."

I roll my eyes. "That's not necessary."

This time, he's brought the condom.

He rolls it on as I hop out of my panties.

Then he picks me up and turns, pressing my back to the door as I wrap my legs around his torso. Yes, he's definitely put on muscle weight since the summer. My thighs have a lot more to squeeze against now.

"Then you're damn well going to come first," he growls as he works his cock against my pussy. I'm so wet, the head of his cock slips right in, and then the weight of my body bearing down pulls the rest of him into me.

The stretch is incredible. Like I wasn't ready, except I was, I am, I love how he displaces that ache I've felt all day with a perfect feeling of being *stuffed*.

"Your fucking pussy," he growls, which I take as a compliment. "Touch your clit. Show me how you get yourself off when you're lonely for this dick."

"I don't," I lie.

He squeezes my hips tight, holding himself inside me, and he pulls me off the door.

Shrieking, I hold on tighter to his shoulders as he turns us again, so he's leaning back against the door and I'm dangerously, precariously bouncing on his cock.

He pumps his hips, thrusting into me, and giving me his thighs to rest on at the same time. "You just forget about sex in between our hookups?"

"Not entirely."

"But mostly."

"Just fuck me, Garrett," I pant.

"Your pussy is clenching me. Try not to come before I get the truth out of you."

"What truth?"

"How many times have you come for me since the last time I had my fingers on your clit?"

"A few." And even admitting that makes me coil tight, like it's too much to reveal, but I can't resist his rough demands.

"This week?"

I flush with reckless heat. "Last weekend. Woke up horny."

"Should've called me."

I shake my head.

"Had to wait until your pussy was this fucking needy?" He strokes into me again, the head of his cock pressing in exactly the right spot. Over and over again.

I guess I did have to wait, because the price of getting fucked this good is having all my secrets laid bare.

I whisper his name, desperate now. My thighs clench against his sides, my toes finding purchase against the door as he arches his back, sliding down a few inches until I'm almost on top of him, both of us desperately working hard to make the other person come.

He wins.

I go first, slamming myself down on his cock and shouting his name. Then he follows, and that feels like I win, too.

We both win…until he's walking himself back to be upright, until I'm hanging in his arms, and it's all too close and intimate and messy.

"Hang on," he sighs as I try to vault my way out of his arms and almost trip. He catches me by the waist, steadying me. "Let me deal with the condom."

At least this time, I'm still wearing his flannel shirt, so covering up is easy.

God, it's annoying how good he makes me feel on a cellular level.

He goes to the bathroom, still shirtless.

I find his Henley and pick it up for him, holding it out so he can grab it when he comes back.

"I know when I'm being dismissed," he says dryly. "You working tomorrow?"

"Yep. Second last shift before—" I cut myself off.

Three days from now, I'm heading home. *We're* heading home, I guess, but separately. I wasn't expecting that for him, because he always spends the holidays with my family, and obviously, he's not invited to that this year.

"Are you driving?"

I swallow hard. "Yeah."

He searches my face, his gaze dark and stormy. "You don't need to pay for the extra insurance on a rental, remember. That fancy black credit card of yours—"

"I know," I say thickly.

I'm not going to tell him I'm not renting a car, because

I've finally bought wheels of my own—that would open a whole different can of worms.

And none of it is his business.

I'm not his to worry about anymore.

"All right." He cups my face in his hand. It smells like me. *He* smells like me, and my heart twists hard. "If you need to get away from the Minelli madness, hit me up. I'll be around."

I don't lean into his touch.

But I don't pull away, either. "Who are you staying with?"

"I'll probably couch surf."

He has five cousins in Pine Harbour. They're all older than us, and married, but Kincaids tend to have open door policies because they had to raise each other. Not having any living parents involved changes how they celebrate the holidays.

My family makes a Big Fucking Deal about Christmas.

The Kincaids—all of them first responders—often volunteer to work over the holidays so other families can be together.

"Then we probably wouldn't be able to meet up in secret, so..."

"We did all right in my truck in September." He drops his hand but doesn't step away. His eyes are full of questions.

"Yeah, that was hot."

"We didn't even have time to fight." He clears his throat. "I've got a theory that we do best in ninety-minute chunks of time."

I laugh weakly. "Oh, yeah?"

He shrugs. "Although I'd convinced myself you decided zero minutes was even better than an hour and a half."

Because I managed not to text him in November. "Ah. Well... I don't always make good choices. Not that this wasn't a good choice. It was... festive."

"Festive." He says it flat.

"Very festive."

He pokes his tongue in his cheek. "Mm."

"Anyway..." That's enough talking probably.

Garrett clearly doesn't agree. "Why'd you go radio silent?"

I make a face. How do I explain that there's a fine line between having a bad day and wanting a distraction—his dick—and...whatever permanent version of Stressville I'm finding myself in this fall?

But I don't need to, because he guesses.

He frowns. "How often are you sleeping at the hospital?"

And right on cue, my pager goes off.

Seeing Garrett's face shut down because I'm pulled into work is all the reminder I need that I'm not right for him, so it doesn't matter how much I miss him in my bed—we *are* only good together for ninety-minute increments. And that's no way to try to maintain a relationship, let alone build a marriage.

"Sorry," I mutter.

"Don't be." He sighs. "I know the drill. Go do your thing. And I'll see you soon. Or not."

"Maybe in the new year," I manage to say before quickly glancing at my pager.

By the time I look up, the door is swinging shut, and Garrett is gone.

Chapter 6

Garrett

I don't even know why I'm going home for Christmas.

Home.

Technically, sure. Pine Harbour is my hometown. It's where I was raised by my dad—if you can call benign neglect by an alcoholic single father who drank himself to an early death *raising*—and it's where I fell in love at the too-young-to-know-better age of sixteen.

But as soon as Rory left, I followed.

And for the next twelve years, I thought of Rory as my home.

Ironic, then, that the last gift I have to wrap, the one I don't really want to wrap, is for her.

The cardboard box sat on my shitty secondhand coffee table until I finished packing everything else. It's something I ordered for Rory in October, didn't have a chance to give her in November, and decided—selfishly—not to give her three days ago.

Now it's taunting me.

Jesus, I'm not looking forward to this week.

That's probably why I'm dawdling. It's not like I had

that much wrapping to do. I have a bag of gifts for my cousins' kids, and a few bottles of booze that's only available in Quebec to soften my couch-surfing request when I get there.

Maybe if shit gets too depressing, I'll sleep in my truck at my cousin Josh's garage.

There's also a nice cutting board for Rory's parents wrapped up, too, in case we cross paths. Just because they're my ex-in-laws doesn't mean I forget how much they all love Christmas. Since I fucking don't, if I'm going to buy presents, I'll include the people who do. And if I don't see them, well...it's probably time I outfit the kitchen in this studio apartment a bit better than the dollar-store basics I bought nine months ago.

As I'm reaching for the wrapping paper, I get a weather alert on my phone. After a week of above seasonal temps, the rest of Ontario is finally getting some snow. Pine Harbour might get a white Christmas after all.

Rory will love that.

But she won't love the drive.

Frowning, I fire off a quick message, hoping it sounds casual.

> Are you on the highway or did you take the backroads? Looks like a storm is rolling in across Toronto.

Then I finish wrapping her present and shove it in the bag with the cutting board for her parents.

By the time I have everything in the truck, I give in to the need to check to see if she's read my messages. Because Dr. Rory Minelli, Chief Fucking Resident, and the smartest person I've ever met, has her read receipts turned on.

Something I usually enjoy, watching that *delivered*

notification turn to *read*. I can practically hear her overactive brain whirring from the other side of Little Italy as she tries to decide how to reply to me.

But today isn't like the other night, or in the summer. This isn't...horny Garrett concern. This is just human being Garrett concern.

And she hasn't read my text message.

She only wants one thing from you, dude, and it isn't a weather report.

That doesn't stop me from glancing at my phone again.

I tap my thumb against the steering wheel of my truck. Of course she isn't going to open my messages—she isn't in heat.

Swearing under my breath, because I've promised myself I wouldn't do this, I swipe into her contact card.

The smartest woman I know also still shares her location with me. It's reckless. It means she hasn't thought about it at all, isn't being careful. It isn't right that I can find out at a glance where she is.

And one of these days, if I look at the wrong time, I'll see her somewhere I wouldn't want to know about—like on a date, or at the house of someone new.

But this morning, she's still at home.

I frown. She hates driving in the dark, and she should have left three hours ago if she wanted to make it to Pine Harbour before dusk.

Me too, but I don't mind night drives.

I put the truck in gear, but I don't head for the highway. I'll just swing by her house and offer to convoy drive, so she isn't alone for that last hour.

I tell myself it's just the nice thing to do. A holiday kindness. But I know the truth. I want to see her, even if it hurts.

I'll always want to see Rory, even if it wrecks me every

time. I will do anything, take any opportunity, to cross paths with the only woman I've ever loved, even if she doesn't love me back anymore.

I follow the location dot for her phone and find her in the small parking lot behind her building. It's deserted this morning, everyone either at work or gone for the holidays already.

I park my truck right beside where she's standing next to an older model hatchback I've never seen before, another slice of the life she's building without me.

She turns, and her shoulders slump.

I step out and slam the door shut harder than I mean to. The wind bites at my face. It's cold as hell and getting colder.

"Battery?" I ask, nodding toward the car.

She doesn't meet my gaze as she sighs and tucks her hands into her coat pocket. "Won't even turn over."

"Pop the hood for me." I open it, check the terminals. Corroded. Her battery's toast. I already know it won't jump, but I try anyway. She's watching me and I need something to do with my hands, anything other than touching her.

The seconds tick by.

"Should I go and get a new battery?" she finally asks.

"It's not just the battery."

"But should I maybe try that?"

I roll my eyes.

"Yeah." I jerk my head at the truck. "Get in."

She snaps her little back super straight. "Excuse me?"

"I'll take you to the store if you think a new battery is all you need."

"I'm fine on my own."

"Yeah? What are you going to do, call an Uber? And

then install the battery yourself? If that *did* work, you still wouldn't get home until midnight."

"Don't yell at me," she snaps.

Which is all the invitation I need to raise my voice. "Why the fuck didn't you tell me you bought a car? Did you even get it properly checked out?"

"Because you'd act like this!"

"Like the fucking thing needs to be re-certified before you take it on the road? You're fucking right I would." I drag my hand over my face, then twist and put my entire attention on closing the hood of her car.

Carefully.

"I don't need your help," she says, her voice small.

"I know you don't," I say. I'm so fucking tired. "When are you coming back?"

"I'm just going up for a few days. I can get Josh to look at it once I'm there, though."

There's no way she's getting the car fixed and driving it all the way to Pine Harbour. "I've got room in the truck."

She stares at me like I just offered to perform open-heart surgery in the parking lot. "What?"

"I'll drive you."

Silence.

"You got someone else heading that way?"

She frowns. "No."

"Then get in the truck."

"But we can't—" She's so righteous when she's mad. Her eyes blaze. "It's eight hours trapped in a small space with me."

"I'll survive."

"What about your ninety-minute max?"

"Get in the truck, Rory."

She stares at me like I'm a stranger, and not the guy who

has done this exact drive with her a couple dozen times before. A whole war goes on behind her snappish eyes, and logic wins out, but she's not happy about it.

I make room for her stuff, a familiar game of Tetris that fills the remaining space in the truck cab and pushes a lot of inconvenient déjà vu buttons.

Now it feels like a drive home for the holidays. All those wintery road trips I complained about, because I didn't get the big deal about a time of year that had never been special for me.

But Rory loves Christmas. *Loves* it.

She gets in and buckles her seatbelt. Then she pulls her toque lower and exhales like this whole ride is a bad idea.

She's probably right.

I put the truck in gear.

She's not looking at me, but I catch her reflection in the window. She looks tired. That deep-in-the-bone exhaustion I remember from when her call shifts used to run over. Back then, I'd have food waiting when she got home.

"I have snacks," I offer. "Healthy ones, even."

No response.

So I add, "You can nap if you want."

"I'm fine."

"Suit yourself. Eight hours ahead of us."

"Don't remind me," she mutters under her breath.

"I think we'll survive."

"Don't be so confident."

"Last I checked, a little arguing hasn't killed anyone. Besides, it's better to get it out of our system now than have it come up while we're trapped in the same small town for a week."

She stiffens. "Wait—how long are you staying?"

Zero to sixty. We didn't even get out of the parking lot.

"It's a figure of speech. I know you've got to be back in a couple days. I'll head back whenever you need to. It's not like I want to spend that much time up there, anyway."

She flicks the briefest of glances my way. "I know it's not your favourite time of year."

"Yeah." I shrug. "Plus, I'm not really looking forward to having to explain all this."

"Explain what?"

"Uh... Us? The reason I need to crash on an available Kincaid couch?"

"You haven't told them?" She sounds shocked.

"No." God, the way my neck just tightened up. And nobody's asked after Rory, either, in months, so I guess everyone just agrees that it makes sense we're done. "It went okay with your folks?"

She doesn't answer. Just stares out the window.

My pulse picks up. "Rory? You did tell them, right?"

"No," she admits finally.

Jesus. "Have you told anyone?"

She shakes her head.

"Not even your sisters?"

"God, no."

"We broke up in *April*."

"And I was heading into my final year of residency," she snaps. "Work is literally all I have time for."

I'm painfully aware of that fact. My cock wants to point out a few highlight moments where she made exceptions to that rule, but...there was also a stretch in there were we couldn't even convince her to take orgasm breaks.

I try to drag in a deep breath, but my chest is too damn tight. I exhale carefully, drumming my thumb against the steering wheel. "Okay, fair. I guess I've been treading water, too."

She gestures toward my lap, which doesn't help with the thickening going on in my jeans. "You've changed plenty."

I don't like the edge in her voice. She's teasing, but she's not.

"So what if I have?" I snap, more defensive than I mean to be.

She backpedals a little. "It's great. I'm saying it's great. Clearly, this whole breakup thing is working for you. You got jacked. You started playing rugby."

That makes me laugh. "Those are the same thing. It's one new hobby. I'm still the same guy, Rory. I still *feel* the same."

And like usual, she doesn't have a reply for that.

After a long, silent pause, I glance over. "You worried about what people are going to say?"

"Of course. You are, too."

"I didn't say that. I said I didn't really know how to explain it."

She makes a deeply frustrated sound I know far too well and jerks her head away, looking out the window.

Drum drum drum. I press my thumb hard against the wheel. "I'll wear it, don't worry."

"That's not how it works." She crosses her arms tighter and hunches up her shoulders. "You're going to come off like the good guy who tried to hang in there while I gave everything to my training, and I'll catch flack for a breakup I didn't even ask for."

She's not wrong. It was my stupid fucking idea. I couldn't keep living in the limbo of being together but never moving forward. Not when she never looked up from her work long enough to notice I was right in front of her, just... waiting.

But her family will only see her ambition and long hours, and decide she ran me off.

She didn't. She was happy enough, even though she was never actually *happy*. We broke up because *I* wanted more and she didn't have anything left to give. Not because she's a workaholic, but because I didn't know how to exist around that. And *that's* on me.

"I'll make it clear," I say quietly.

"I thought about telling them every time I called home, you know. But the words never came out."

"Yeah." I try to grab at any lifeline I can offer her here. "The holidays are probably as good a time as any to break it to them. With all your aunts visiting."

Rory's aunts are a *lot*.

She doesn't respond, and we drive in silence after that. The city gives way to the highway, then the highway gives way to county roads with frozen marsh on one side and steep, blasted rocks on the other.

The minutes tick by.

The playlist I was listening to when she got in—quiet '70s rock—finally ends.

I clear my throat. "You want to pick something?"

She blinks at me, clearly lost in thought.

"You don't have to," I say. "Just figured it's fair to take turns."

"So I can put on a holiday playlist?"

"I don't hate Christmas music."

"Sure," she says sarcastically. "You only grumble every time it comes on and roll your eyes at all the overplayed stuff."

"No grumbling today. No eye rolling, either."

"I literally have a playlist called *Overplayed Christmas Music*. You're saying I can put that on?"

I bite down on the inside of my cheek. "Yeah, go for it."

"I'm just kidding, by the way. That's not what the list is called." She reaches for the display screen to switch from my phone to her phone—something she's done dozens of times before.

Except her phone isn't in the saved devices list, because I deleted it.

"Sorry," I say gruffly as her fingers pause just above the screen.

She takes a deep breath. "Do you mind if I pair again?"

I gesture for her to go ahead.

She taps the buttons, and then—fuck me—my truck recognizes her phone again, because she's still in my phonebook.

Neither of us say anything as the display flashes a message. ***My Favourite Person's Phone is now connected.***

My heart hammers in my chest.

Quietly, she clears her throat, then ducks her head and starts scrolling for something for us to listen to.

The first song is definitely overplayed. Definitely something I would roll my eyes at. But as it starts playing, as I can feel her staring at the display, I know I'll remember this moment every time I hear it in the future. Rory tightening up, her pretty face going blank, like she needs a mask to get through just being in my truck again.

I'll remember the hurt I've caused her, and the stupid unspoken rules that seem to be developing between us.

Only once a month—if I'm lucky.

Only for ninety minutes.

No talking after.

No kissing, but everything else we can fit in that brief window of time. Absolutely anything and everything.

The sex has never been hotter, and I fucking hate it. I mean, I don't hate it enough to stop, because I also love it, crave it, need it more than my next breath.

But fuck, I wish everything was different.

And now a fucking Christmas song is going to remind me of every mistake I made that led me to this moment.

The next song sears into my skin, too. Probably the whole playlist of Christmas pop music is going to be trauma-imprinted on my soul by the time we get to Pine Harbour.

Then, somewhere in the middle of song four, without looking at me, Rory murmurs, "It's hard not being your favourite person anymore."

The words hit like a sledgehammer.

I'm not sure what's worse—her thinking that she's not anymore, because of course she still is, or the weight of knowing that I'll never get to say that out loud. That's my secret to carry now, and it's so fucking heavy.

Instead, I grip the steering wheel and try not to think about the way her voice cracked on that last word. Try not to remember the last time we made this drive together, my arm draped over the console, her bare knee pressed against my knuckles, singing along to the radio like we were the two happiest people in the world.

Now we're just two liars, driving home to a family that thinks we're still that happy.

God damn it.

As if Rory is stewing over the same thoughts, she suddenly asks, "So... what's the plan when we get there?"

I try not to tense up, but I think she can feel my *I don't fucking know* reaction.

She takes a deep breath. "Because I was thinking—what if we, um... broke up again?"

Chapter 7

Rory

Garrett looks at me like I've got two heads. "Pardon?"

"You said it yourself; you don't know how to explain our breakup."

"I don't *want* to explain it," he growls. "It's not anyone's business but ours."

"I agree."

"So we should just tell people that."

I can't agree with that. "It won't work."

"Why not?"

"They won't believe us."

"That's too bad for them, because it's pretty fucking real."

I rub my chest. Don't I know it. "Just hear me out."

"About a staged breakup?" He makes a face. "Once wasn't enough for you?"

I ignore that dig.

"It might be easier," I say, sounding more uncertain than I'd like.

"Easier for...?"

"Well... My parents, for one. If they...see it, then they won't question it."

"So you think we should lie to them?"

"We haven't been honest with them in months," I snap. "If anything, this is just correcting an assumption."

He doesn't respond to that, which pushes my internal panic index into the danger zone. "Garrett, I can't handle the constant questioning and lecturing from my family. You know what they're like. If we don't make it crystal clear, then the entire visit will be spent explaining what happened, over and over again. Not just explaining, but having to justify it. They won't believe that I did enough to try and save our—"

I cut myself off, because I probably didn't do enough to save our relationship. But neither did Garrett. We just let it slip away, and that's a regret I'll have for the rest of my life, because he was—is—so important to me.

But I didn't grieve the loss of him for eight long months only to re-hash it all with my parents.

If I wanted their opinions about it, I'd have told them sooner.

"Never mind," I manage to stammer out. "Fine, we can do it your way."

And he just nods.

I want to cry.

I won't, though. I have more control over myself than that. So I drill all my attention into picking better holiday songs, weird stuff that maybe Garrett hasn't heard before, or stuff that I know he likes, like "Fairytale of New York" by The Pogues.

Over the next hour and a half, we listen to an eclectic mix. But we don't fight again, and he doesn't side-eye any of the songs. His thumb even starts tapping along to some.

It's a minor road trip victory.

"You hungry?" he asks suddenly.

Right on cue, my stomach growls. "Um, maybe."

He shifts slightly in his seat and jerks his thumb back to the cooler.

I twist and open the lid, looking at his picnic. There's a massive wrap that looks like it's got turkey and spinach on it, as well as some apple slices and clementines, which surprise me. I love clementines, they're my fave, but he's never been a fan before.

The wrap looks like he pre-cut it in half, so we could share that.

"Turkey, you say?"

"It's good, I promise."

"I believe you." I grab it, as well as two clementines, which I let roll into the cup holders between us before I take half the wrap out of the Ziplock bag.

Up close, it's not just a *turkey and spinach* wrap. It's like a chopped salad with spinach, red pepper, celery, and other veggies, dressed and neatly folded inside turkey breast and a whole wheat wrap.

I stare at it. "There are vegetables in here."

Garrett muffles a laugh. "Correct."

"You made this?"

"Correct again."

I narrow my eyes. "That's not treading water."

"You sound suspicious."

"You just randomly swung by to see me this morning?"

"I wouldn't say randomly. But I didn't pack a delicious sandwich in the great hope that you might need to get in my truck and eat half of it, if that's what you're thinking. I promise, you, Roar, if I thought we'd have ended up road tripping together today, I'd have vacuumed out the cab and packed a second sandwich for you so you didn't have to eat half of mine."

"I don't have to eat it." I shove it across to him.

He doesn't take it.

"That's what you heard?" He sighs and shakes his head. "I just would have made you something without spinach because I know it's not your favourite."

Oh.

"Thank you," I whisper. The lump gets bigger so that's all I get out.

"I'm still the jerk who broke up with you," he says gruffly. "Don't go being soft on me."

I take a bite of his wrap and shake my head.

"I won't," I mumble around the deliciousness.

We've just finished the wrap when we see a sign for a coffee shop a few minutes ahead.

"Might as well stop and stretch our legs, yeah?" Garrett asks.

It's where we usually stop, after all.

I nod and start gathering up the wrappers to toss when we get out.

Inside, there's a crowd of travellers all thinking the same thing as us. The line up for the men's room goes faster than the ladies', though, and by the time I get out, Garrett's already ordered and he's holding two coffee cups at the door.

"Mocha or double-double?" He holds up one cup, then the other, giving me a choice of my two favourite coffee orders.

"Thank you," I mutter, reaching for the mocha. He's already holding it out, knowing that's the one I'll pick, and my fingers don't just meet the cup but wrap around his hand, too.

My breath catches at the visceral flashback, the odd déjà vu of it all, and from the low grunt he makes, I think he's also remembering other times we've stopped here on drives home.

The memories surge as we climb back into the truck.

Last winter, neither of us had heard "Last Christmas" by Wham yet, so we spent the entire drive listening to the radio in a hilarious game of Whamaggedon Chicken. We'd leave it on a station for a few songs and then switch to a new one, always holding our breath as we scrolled lest we accidentally stumbled across it.

We didn't hear it once that drive, and we were grinning from ear to ear when we arrived at my parents' house—only to hear them listening to it as we walked in the door.

"So close," Garrett whispered in my ear, his breath hot against my skin. "We definitely get a consolation prize, right?"

The consolation prize was very quiet mutual masturbation orgasms, because my childhood bed squeaks, and my parents are—were—fine with us sleeping in the same room, but I don't need them to know we have—had—sex under their roof.

After putting his coffee cup in the cupholder, displacing the clementine I dropped there, Garrett cranks the heat and we get back on the road.

The first winter he had this truck, we pulled off to the side of the road and had a frantic quickie because I'd been so busy with exams the week before we left it had been a while, and I knew I wouldn't want to have sex once we got home.

I take a big sip of my mocha trying to chase *that* memory away.

It's hot on my tongue, a little uncomfortable, but the

distraction works—for a moment. More memories cascade into the void, though. Like the year we realized halfway home that we'd forgotten all of the presents, and we stopped at a Giant Tiger and did our best.

Buying last minute discount presents for everyone was the highlight of the entire holidays that year. The way we laughed, the way we hyped up every mediocre choice, convincing each other it would be loved by the recipient.

Damn damn damn.

I pretend to scroll through my phone to avoid watching him. His hand is on the gearshift, and I have a sudden, stupid flash of how he used to rest that same hand on my thigh during long drives. Just because he could. Just because he liked to touch me.

And I liked it too.

I'm not allowed to like it anymore.

"You got any more songs on that playlist?" Garrett's sudden question breaks the silence.

"I didn't realize it had stopped."

"We could listen to the radio?" He turns it on and gets static. "Think we'll get lucky and avoid—"

The chorus of "Last Christmas" interrupts him as he lands on the first station after pressing search.

"No luck for us this year, I guess," I mutter.

He turns the radio off again.

"Hey, you can stay asleep if you want. I just gotta stretch my legs." Garrett's voice drifts through the muzzy heaviness of a blissful nap.

I blink my eyes open. It's dark outside, and when I blearily focus on what's outside the truck window, I realize we're less than two hours from home. "Shit, how long was I asleep?"

"A couple hours."

I push myself to sit up, my stiff muscles protesting. "I should pee, too. And it's my turn to get coffee."

He hops out and comes around to my side of the truck, waiting for me as I stretch and get blood flowing to my sleep-heavy limbs again.

"Let me guess, you worked nonstop for the last week to carve out this vacation time," he says as we hurry across the parking lot to the rest stop.

I would shrug if I wasn't shivering so hard against the cold. I work nonstop every week. "Thanks for letting me nap."

"Yeah, of course." He grabs the door and holds it for me, frowning.

"What?"

"Nothing."

And then we go our separate ways into the washrooms.

I come out first, so I get in line for coffee. He joins me before I get to the cash. "Do you want anything else?"

He shakes his head. "I'm good."

We step forward, and I place our order. After I pay, and we move down the counter to grab the drinks, he says, "I want to ask how work is going."

I immediately bristle.

He sighs. "Yeah, I didn't think you wanted to talk about it."

"It's complicated."

"Sure. I get that." I hate how understanding his smile is.

Understanding, but sad, and it doesn't go anywhere near his eyes.

"Double-double and a decaf mocha?" Our order is called out.

"That's us." I snatch mine and whirl away.

Garrett doesn't catch up until we're at the truck.

As I bundle myself into the passenger side, he peels off his parka and gets the truck turned on. Where I like to wear my warm coat the whole drive, he prefers to drive in just his shirt, even though his breath is visible until the heater catches up.

Once we're back on the road, he brings it up again.

"I get that your work is off-limits," he says, his eyes never leaving the road. "But when it's the only thing you care about, it makes small talk...hard."

I don't bother to argue the point that it's the only thing I care about. I won't win that fight.

"Nobody said we had to make small talk," I mutter.

"Touché."

"This road trip was your idea," I point out.

"Because I know how important it is to you to get home for Christmas."

Something about the way he says that takes my breath away, makes me all hot and furious inside. "So magnanimous!"

"Come on, Roar, you didn't have another option, and I was right there."

"I could've rented a car."

He snorts. "You think there are any rental cars left? Tomorrow is Christmas Eve."

Deep down, I know that.

But I still bristle. "Why did you come to check on me?"

"You really want to pick a fight about me trying to be a good friend?"

"Maybe. Yes." I sigh. "No."

He nods. Then he groans. "I don't know how to turn off the part of my brain that thinks about you. You, uh, still have your location shared with me. I was checking to see where you were on the road, and when I saw that you hadn't left yet, I knew there was a problem. And when there's a problem for you, Rory, there's a problem for me."

Hot tears press against the inside of my eyelids. I wish his desire to fix my problems didn't extend to a need to fix *me*, too.

"I don't even know why we fight anymore," I say, after a long stretch of silence. "Half the time I'm not sure what we're even fighting about sometimes."

Garrett shoots me a surprised look. "Yeah," he says slowly. "Like we just keep picking up an old fight that we never finished?"

That feels surprisingly accurate. We never got closure on our breakup. We went from raw emotion to a cold agreement that we needed a break so fast, there was no processing time. And then it was painfully polite, like a Cold War, followed by heated clashes that turned sexy every time instead of actually resolving anything.

"It's not as if we had a lot of practice arguing," I muse out loud. "We didn't fight this much when we were together. I mean, before those last couple months."

His jaw flexes. "Is that how you remember it?"

I blink. "Do you remember it differently? When did we fight?"

His body tenses, his shoulders hunching up around his ears. His hands grip the steering wheel so tight, his forearms flex.

"Only like... every four years." He says flatly. "Or five, in this case."

I frown. "What do you mean, once every four or five years?"

"Every time you finished another chunk of your school, Roar, you moved the goalposts. And when it happened again and again, I started to feel like everything we had agreed upon to that point was a lie."

"A lie?" Oh, this, this feels real. This feels raw, but we're getting somewhere now. Yes, we *do* need closure on this, apparently, because I *never* lied to him, ever.

I swallow hard, staring out at the frozen highway unfolding ahead of us.

My throat tightens, but I don't cry. Not yet. But God, we are long overdue for this fight. And maybe, finally, for what comes after it. My voice is barely above a whisper. "I never lied to you. You knew. You knew, from before we started dating. You knew when I was seventeen that I wanted to be a doctor."

"And you knew I wanted to get married."

I'm struck speechless.

His voice drops low. "How many times did I ask you when I could propose? When I could ask you to marry me, and you would say yes?"

"You asked me that when we were *kids*."

"And you said, when you finished university. And I took that to mean your undergraduate program. So you get your degree, you have graduation, and it's a big fucking moment. And I know better. I know not to make that moment about us, because that moment is entirely about you. I know that, and I am so fucking proud of you, but there was a small part of me that, deep down, was like, yes, fucking finally, now we can talk about the future. Except when I tried, you said, ahhh, maybe after medical school. Do you remember? And then we had the same conversation again when you were looking at residencies. There was never any space in our relationship to talk about how fucking earth shattering it felt for *me* when every conversation about marriage was pushing it off into the future—"

"But I didn't say," I interrupt him, because this isn't fair. "I didn't say, you couldn't ask me to—I never said I didn't want to get engaged. It was just a wedding that I thought we should wait on. And I don't remember fighting about any of that."

"We didn't." He growls low under his breath. "We fought about other stuff, and then you would get into the groove of a new program, a new rotation, a new placement, and it would all be forgotten."

"By me, but apparently not by you." My chest hurts. "Is that why we never got engaged?"

The question catches at something inside me. Because, yeah—maybe we weren't officially engaged, but we felt engaged. We were *us*. All the way through med school. And when I got my residency in the same city, it felt like the universe was finally giving us a clear path to a home and a future for our little family of two.

"Garrett... I didn't know."

"Yeah. That's on me. I never told you. Because the time was never right and the goalposts kept moving. But most of the time, I was happy and so it was fine."

My heart lodges in my throat. "So what changed?"

"At some point this past year... I realized *you* weren't happy. And that was unbearable."

Chapter 8

Garrett

The rest of the drive is completely silent.

I know I shouldn't have said all of that, but especially the part about her not being happy. As the words tumbled out, she practically crawled inside herself, getting smaller inside her puffy winter coat, turning her face to the dark window.

There's such a thing as too much honesty.

Fuck.

But what's done is done.

I need to find a way to salvage the holidays for her. Rory loves Christmas, her whole family loves Christmas and goes over the top for it. I forced her into my truck and made her to talk about something that should be left as water under the bridge—done and dusted months ago.

As we pass the sign on the highway that Pine Harbour is ahead, I say, "I'll come in with you. I'll tell them that we're not together anymore, and I'll one hundred percent take the responsibility. I won't leave until they accept that."

"Oh, great," she says, staring out the window. "Just how I want my Christmas holidays to begin—with an awkward and frustrating conversation." She pauses. "But it'll be good to rip the Band-aid off, and then go our separate ways."

Rip the Band-aid off, I repeat to myself.

We turn off the highway. Mac's Diner is lit up, and the parking lot is full. Maybe I'll loop back there to grab dinner after I drop Rory off.

Main Street is quiet, all the stores closed now for the night.

At the end of the main drag there's a hill that separates the town from the harbour itself. During the day, we'd see the wild, frigid waves of Lake Huron crashing against the shore, but now that it's dark, the lake is just an endless stretch of darkness.

Like we're driving to the edge of the world.

Growing up, that's what it felt like for sure.

At the bottom of the hill, at the T-junction of Main Street and Old Whiskey Harbour Road—officially just Harbour Road now but nobody who grew up in Pine Harbour calls it that —is my cousin Josh's garage. Across from it is the marina, and behind that is a long-abandoned motel that features a new "Re-opening soon!" sign. A spark of progress in our little hometown.

Behind the garage, across from the motel, is another new business, the Pine Harbour Brewery.

And then there's nothing but forest.

We curve south along the lake. A drive I've done hundreds of times, starting in high school when I'd wait for Rory after class just for a chance to give her a ride home.

This might be the last time I ever deposit her on the doorstep at the Pine Harbour Little Tree Farm.

My throat squeezes tight.

I can feel her tensing up, too. And I know why. Her parents are going to open the door and smile like everything's fine, like their eldest daughter is home with her steadfast boyfriend. As if *we* are still a singular unit. *Rory and Garrett are here!*

RoryandGarrett.

That's what we've been for more than a decade.

No wonder she hasn't told them yet.

There are two entrances to the farm. The first one is for the public, and as we pass it, I can see the lights strung up throughout the rows of Christmas trees are still on, so someone is working the stand.

One less person to worry about telling in person. But also, one less person who will hear it from me, ergo making them Rory's problem alone.

Her mom opens the front door before we even make it to the porch. The golden glow from inside spills out onto the snow, warm and inviting. Damn it. I don't want to miss this farm. I don't want to think about the memories attached to this place.

I follow Rory, her backpack in one hand, my gift for the Minellis in the other, ready to execute my plan: *Merry Christmas, we broke up, it's amicable, here's a nice cutting board.* Then I'm gone.

The plan disintegrates before we even step across the threshold.

"I should warn you," Carmen Minelli says to Rory, her voice low. "Your sister's just arrived and she's upset."

"Jules?"

Carmen shakes her head. "She's not getting in until tomorrow. *Cassie* is here."

I slow to a stop behind them. Cassandra, the middle Minelli daughter, lives just outside of Pine Harbour with her husband, Nate, a helicopter pilot. He's a decade older than her and Rory had misgivings when her younger sister got married, but I thought they were happy.

Carmen lowers her voice even further, but I still catch her words. "And she's *alone*."

Rory races ahead. I'm right behind her, and my heart sinks as I watch her clock the miserable tableau in the kitchen.

Cassie leaning against the counter, mascara streaking down her cheek, their father hovering helplessly with a dish towel. An oversized, overstuffed suitcase next to the entrance to the hallway.

Rory spins around and gives me a desperate, pleading look I've only seen a handful of times over the last ten years. "Garrett, babe, can you take our bags upstairs?"

Babe?

Our bags?

Fuck me.

"I need a minute with my sister," she adds, her voice tightening up, as if she's worried that I might bail on her.

Probably because I told her that her unhappiness was unbearable, and now her entire family is unhappy at the supposed-to-be happiest time of the year.

Part of me resents that she doesn't know I'd help out in this moment. That she doesn't know I still care about her needs. *Haven't I fucking shown that over the last four months?*

And it's not like she's shown a fucking moment of caring about *my* needs.

What *I* need is to get in my truck and drive to my cousin's place. I need distance and boundaries and probably several beers. So *no*, I can't take *our* bags upstairs, because where the fuck am I going to put them?

Her bedroom?

Like that won't absolutely wreck me.

Because the only end game on *this* playing out is us pretending that we're still together, which means falling asleep next to Rory and waking up next to Rory and—

But from the look on her face, what I need doesn't matter.

"Yeah, sure," I say slowly. *You wanted to save Christmas for her, you fucking chump. This is how you save Christmas for her.*

Her shoulders drop slightly in relief.

"I'll, um, come up in a minute? Just need to..." She gestures vaguely at her sister.

"Of course."

Her dad grabs onto the lifeline of escape. "I'll help bring stuff in from the truck."

"No, I've got it—" I start to say, but he's already heading outside.

So I take what I've got in my hands already and escape up the familiar stairs.

I dump Rory's backpack on the same double bed where we lost our virginity at seventeen, then put the wrapped cutting board on her little desk where we prop up her computer so we can watch stand-up comedy as we fall asleep. It still has the same faded periodic table poster pinned above it. Our matching Christmas bathrobes from last year, a gift from Cassie and Jules, are still hanging on the back of the bedroom door.

Everything is the exact same...except us.

"What do you got in these bags, Garrett?" Rory's dad pushes his way into the room and plunks down the totes full of Christmas presents for my cousins and their kids.

Apparently *I've got it* means nothing.

Bottles of booze to buy off people I was planning to beg

for couch space, I want to say. I hope he didn't notice the sleeping bag, aka my backup plan.

Instead I say, "I've got the rest."

He nods, and doesn't move anywhere.

Ah, fuck. More Minelli emotional chaos, incoming.

"Hell of a thing," he says quietly. "They seemed so happy just a few days ago."

Yeah, I think. *I know the feeling.*

"Did she, uh, say what happened?"

He shakes his head. "She just arrived right before you. We thought her car was your truck, actually." He claps me on the shoulder. "I'm glad you're here, son. You and Rory have always been so steady."

Oh, the painful irony.

When I follow him back downstairs, Rory's wrapped around Cassie, holding her tight.

She looks up at me over her sister's shoulder, then whispers something quietly. Cassie nods, and Rory slips away.

Her hand catches my wrist. Just for a second. Just long enough for her fingers to press against my pulse point and make me yearn in a way I should be used to, but still find catches me off guard every time.

We used *to be so steady.*

"I need to get one more bag from the truck," I mutter under my breath. "Then can we talk?"

She nods. "Upstairs?"

By the time I get up to her room, she's mostly unpacked and is shoving her empty bag under the bed.

I close the door and lean back against it. "What the fuck is going on?"

She sits down on the bed. "Cassie's getting divorced."

"A divorce? They aren't just fighting?"

"She's packed her stuff and is moving home."

"Did she say what happened?"

Rory's gaze drops to the floor. "Um, he works too much and doesn't listen to her."

"Ah."

She takes a deep breath. "I don't think right now is a good time to tell them that we've broken up."

"I got that from you calling me *babe*."

"That wasn't a plan, you know. That was just...I panicked." She runs a hand through her hair, sending dark curls twisting in all directions. "Can you— Can we just take a few minutes here? Please?"

I shove my hands in my pockets. "Yeah, okay."

"They're gonna blame me," she finally says quietly.

I stare at her, incredulous. "How is Cassie's breakup *your* fault?"

"I know my mom's gonna be like, 'Why didn't you see this coming?'"

"Okay, well..." I scrub my brow. I really do love the Minellis—not as much as I love Rory, but her family came with her. It was a package deal, and there was a lot to be said for them. But they're too hard on their oldest daughter. It isn't her fault that her sister got married way too young.

Especially when Rory did the exact opposite. But I'm not going to think about that now.

I scrub my hands over my face. "Well, I was going to suggest that you say you want alone time with Cassie right now, and I'll get out of your hair and go stay somewhere else."

She gives me a panicked look.

"But I get now that would be a bad idea," I add.

I also don't want to lie to Rory's family, though. Because lying to everyone else also drags us into the lie and that's where everything gets murky. It's way too easy to pretend to be important to Rory. A dumb fuck like me could fall for that trap and start to think it's true.

Fucking hell.

"We'll figure this out," I mutter, more to myself than to her.

The door behind me thumps as someone tries to push in.

"Oh, sorry Garrett," Carmen says when I step aside and she bustles in, oblivious to the tension. "Dante said he brought your bag of presents up here. Do you want them under the tree?"

"Not those," I manage to say. "But, uh, this one is for you guys." I grab the wrapped cutting board and hand it over.

"Oh, that's so sweet. Thank you. Are you hungry? You must be exhausted from that drive. Rory said you did it straight through?"

"Yeah, wanted to beat the storm."

"Such a good man." She pats my arm. "Taking care of our girl."

Rory makes a sound that might be agreement or might be choking.

I cover for her by grabbing at random weather small talk. "Storm seems to have fully missed the peninsula, though, eh?"

"We got some fresh flakes this morning, but nothing since then. And the temperature is supposed to go up above freezing tomorrow. Should be a good skating day."

That is genuinely good to hear, I wasn't looking forward to freezing my ass off. But as long as there's a chance I'm going to be stuck helping with the Minelli Christmas Eve tradition, then I might as well have some homecooked food to fuel up. "And I think we're both hungry, yeah."

As soon as her mom leaves, Rory stands up and crosses to me, her eyes wide, her cheeks pink. "Thank you," she whispers under her breath. "I owe you."

Fuck. That look on her face pretty much seals the deal. Time for me to make myself comfy in my ex-girlfriend's childhood bedroom, pretending to be the boyfriend I haven't been for eight months.

"Probably no chance in actually having privacy to talk about this until everyone else turns in for the night, right?"

She winces. "Sorry."

"Yeah."

"Garrett..."

"I know," I say. Because I do.

I know what she needs even when she can't say it. I know when she needs space, and I know when she needs company. I know when she needs me to run interference, or to stand back and let her have a go at something.

I have spent almost fifteen years studying Aurora Minelli's every mood, every whim, every dream, and every despair.

Even if we fell out of love, I can't forget all the ways I consumed her when I did love her with all of my heart.

Because even when we're not together, I'm still hers. Even if it goes against every act of self-preservation I have left.

Fuck.

Tonight is going to be a *long* night in this little room chock full of memories, because there's two of us and only one bed.

Chapter 9

Rory

I'm feeling shell-shocked as we sit down to dinner. Cassie has begged off, claiming she can't bear the thought of food, and has headed over to work at the Christmas tree sales stand.

Minellis burying their feelings under a mountain of work is pretty par for the course.

Dad went with her, so it's just Mom and Garrett and me.

"Nice to have a moment of quiet with just you two before the hordes descend on us tomorrow," she says.

Garrett chuckles. "Do you mean the skaters, or your sisters?"

Christmas Eve is always a busy day for our farm. Growing up, my parents would discount the remaining trees to get them all sold before my mom's sisters and their families all descend upon us.

A couple of years ago, my dad added a skating trail that winds through the forest, and he charges a small entrance fee. Throughout the month of December, families come for a skate and a hot chocolate before they grab a tree to take home. But the day before Christmas, the skating trail is free admission—and he's found that this is a better selling feature than discounting the trees ever was.

Usually, he's sold the last of the trees by lunch time, and the rest of the afternoon is just the hot chocolate stand and maybe some impromptu wreath sales with left over boughs of greenery.

It's my favourite day of the year. There's something magical about it, a real sense of festive community.

Then my aunts arrive and we have a huge feast, followed by everyone "watching Christmas movies" but they're really just background noise as we read books we've swapped with each other. Which is the perfect way to cap the perfect day.

"I mean the skaters," my mom teases right back to Garrett. "I can't wait to see my sisters."

Like us, my mom is one of three girls. Like me, she's the oldest. Unlike me, she loves being the oldest and most responsible. My Aunt Mara is an artist who has one daughter, Glory, who she's raising by herself by choice. And Aunt Tabitha waited until she was in her forties to have kids, so she has two pre-school boys who are hell on wheels.

As if I invoked their names out loud, my mom claps her hands. "Speaking of which, my darlings, I have a big favour to ask of you. Tabby was saying that it might be easier if the boys slept in a room with a door. So I was thinking of putting them in your room. Of course you can sleep there tonight, it's your space until they arrive. But tomorrow night, would you mind bedding down in the back room?"

The back room, aka a sunroom on the back of the farmhouse that my dad winterized, is a sprawling family room style space where we typically open presents on Christmas morning, because there's a nice bar where the grownups can have coffee and breakfast while the heathens—I mean my cousins—tear into all the presents Aunt Tabby will bring for them.

Plus, it has separate couches.

"Sure," Garrett says at the same time as I say, "We could move in there immediately, in fact."

"Oh, no, don't be silly," my mom laughs. "I won't make you sleep apart tonight. And you've already unpacked."

"Only me," I say brightly, about to offer that Garrett could move into the back room immediately when the phone rings.

My mom excuses herself to answer it and Garrett gives me a look across the table.

"Too obvious?" I whisper.

He shrugs. "I'll sleep on the couch if you want to field the questions about that in the morning."

I do *not*.

"I'm not sleeping on the floor, though," he continues. "You know I'm going to have to be one of the safety monitors on the skating trail tomorrow, and I can't be stiff for that."

I narrow my eyes. It's a reasonable point, but there's something in the way he's saying it. "Is this a game of chicken?"

"I'm not afraid to sleep in the same bed as you, Roar." His expression hasn't changed, but his voice...that got low. Private. *Hot*.

I'm staring at him, my cheeks flaming, when my mom comes back. "Eat up, kids. Your dad needs your help with a delivery. Cassie started crying again when your dad told her about it, so..."

"Yeah, sure, I can go," Garrett offers before quickly shovelling a few more bites into his face.

My mom winces. "And she's crying again, so she probably can't be left alone at the stall."

I push my plate in her direction. "Sorry to bail on dishes, then. I'll go keep her company."

"Talk to her, please. I'm worried that she's making a hasty decision."

"I—" My mouth flaps wordlessly for a second.

"Come on, Roar." Garrett grabs my hand and tugs me out of my seat. "These trees won't deliver themselves."

He hustles me into my coat and shoves a random Little Tree Farm toque on my head.

"I'm not going to tell Cassie that she's made a mistake," I snap hotly as soon as we're outside.

"I didn't hear your mom say that you should."

"She called it *hasty*. You don't think that's a loaded term?"

"Yeah, no, you're right." He zips up his coat, then unzips it. "It's not that cold tonight, eh?"

I growl under my breath and stomp faster down the side lane between the house and the public part of the farm.

It's not cold, actually. The wind that blew us all the way here has died down, and in the stillness, you can hear people skating on the trail that winds along parallel to this lane. Laughing, chasing.

Murmuring.

I trip over my feet as I realize people are doing...something...just on the other side of the thick hedge.

"Keep moving," Garrett rumbles in my ear as he catches me and propels me forward.

"I'm fine."

"Of course you are."

"I don't care if people make out on the skate trail."

"Sure."

"I *don't*."

"If anything, you're jealous."

I whirl around on him. "What?"

"Come on, Roar. Your mom's comment got under your skin because of *us*. Not your sister. And we hear people having fun...." He shrugs. "I'm jealous."

"Don't project that on me."

He holds up his hands. "Fine."

"We didn't break up hastily."

"Oh, I'm painfully aware."

But I am very grateful that I didn't show up here alone, in a hatchback with a bad battery, and have to explain why I didn't have the ever-helpful boyfriend in tow.

Dodged a bullet there.

So I'm not going to pick a fight with Garrett when he's ambling along beside me, pretending to be mine even when I'm in a terrible mood.

"Do you want a hot chocolate before you leave with the delivery?" I ask. "A peace offering, if you will."

He bows, exaggerating his gratitude. "I'd love that."

I pick up my pace, speeding ahead of him into the clearing at the public entrance.

I love the tree lot so much. There are a few temporary huts that we re-purpose throughout the year with removable decorative pieces. In the fall, they're pumpkin and apple themed. Throughout December, they're straight out of the North Pole. After the holidays, they'll pivot to a maple sugar bush aesthetic, which stretches the skating trail season all the way to March Break

My dad keeps the delivery truck right at the front gate. It's a classic cherry red pickup that Garrett helped restore when we were in high school.

It has his fingerprints all over it—and so did I, back in the day.

We used to *leap* at the chance to do evening deliveries. We'd race through them as fast as we could to steal some make out time in the community centre parking lot before returning to the farm.

My dad is nowhere in sight, so Garrett turns right to find him deeper in the trees, and I go left to the pop-up coffee stand.

Cassie appears beside me as I'm leaving the counter, two hot chocolates in hand.

"So..." She scuffs her boot against the frozen dirt. And then she bursts into tears.

Oh, shit. "Um..." I wish I wasn't holding the hot chocolates. "Damn it, I can't hug you with my hands full!"

"I'm sorry," she mumbles.

"Let's go to the delivery truck."

She leads the way and opens the driver's door for me. It's a vintage truck with a bench seat, but when they were restoring it, they built in flip-out cup holders. Thank God.

I ditch the hot chocolate and then squeeze my sister again. "Hey, hey, it's okay."

"I know," she says, but she sounds miserable.

"Of course you're sad," I whisper. "Let me just get Garrett out of my hair and then we can talk."

She shakes her head. "I want to help Dad. You go with Garrett on the delivery."

"I don't need to do that." I don't *want* to do that, but I'm not going to dump that on her right now.

"You should." She sucks in a breath. "It's Jake and Dani who want the trees."

Oh.

Dani is our cousin. She's a few years older than me,

happily married to a local contractor, and they have a big house on the outskirts of town.

And Cassie and Nate live just down the street from them. Or, as of this afternoon, maybe just Nate does.

Yikes, what a mess.

"Go," Cassie urges. "And when you get back, we'll open a bottle of wine. Maybe if we get Mom tipsy enough, she won't try to meddle tonight."

Before I can gently suggest that booze may not help, my dad and Garrett appear, each of them carrying a tree.

And somehow I find myself climbing into the passenger seat.

I tell myself it's because I want to see Dani. Growing up we weren't very close—my dad and his brother had a falling out when we were little—but as adults, we've discovered we have a lot in common.

She's a paramedic, and twelve years ago, she moved back home after completing that training when I decided I wanted to set my sights on medical school. She was my biggest cheerleader in that final year of high school, when I was dating Garrett and torn about what universities to apply to, because some of them were really far away.

If he's a good one, he'll follow you wherever you go, she told me.

And he did.

But I fucked it up.

I keep fucking it up, and there aren't enough hot chocolates in the world to fix that.

"What do Jake and Dani want with four more live cut trees?" Garrett asks, interrupting my spinning thoughts as the truck climbs the hill from the harbour, back into town.

"I don't actually know. But their Christmas lights display has gotten bigger and bigger each year."

Garrett turns at the only traffic lights in town, heading north away from Main Street. Older residential blocks lead to the park surrounding a community centre and the community school, and on the other side of that is a newer development. When Jake built his house as a young contractor, it was the only one on this road. Now there's a whole neighbourhood here, and it's walking distance into town.

"It's pretty cool to see how much the town has grown since we lived here," I murmur.

"It's so big Pine Harbour has rush hour now," Garrett jokes.

There *are* a lot of cars ahead of us, even though it's well after the end of regular work hours. And then we pass a homemade, oversized street sign. *Polar Expressway*, it reads. And then below that, *drive slowly and watch for elves.*

"So this is why your dad thought we should make the delivery together." Garrett sighs. "It's a thing, like the horse drawn wagons tomorrow."

I smother a smile. "Thank you for suffering through the overwrought festive fun with me."

He laughs under his breath. "Don't pretend you don't love it. You *always* loved this stuff. Remember the first winter we had this truck for deliveries and you decorated it with battery powered Christmas lights?"

We both fall silent.

Because he'd growled about it being over the top, but after we finished deliveries, he used the strand of lights to hold my wrists together. *My little prisoner*, he whispered. *Kinky*, I whispered back before he kissed me.

And then we had a weirdly wonderful conversation about kink and sex and wanting to learn more about that together.

My throat gets tight.

How disappointed those eighteen-year-olds would be now, to see us at thirty, broken apart and angry.

"We have a lot of memories in this truck," Garrett finally says.

His voice is rough, and his words catch on my own memories. After a long day being together in the enclosed space of *his* truck cab, this one shouldn't feel different. But it is.

"Yeah," I whisper. "If this bench seat could talk, right?"

He eases the truck forward another few feet, then comes to a stop again. Which is just enough time for my pulse to rocket out of control, because why did I say that?

But when he looks at me, and his gaze is hot and sharp and complicated, I know why I said it.

Because it's really fucking hard to actually let Garrett go.

Damn it all to hell.

The roughness smooths out of his voice as he holds my gaze. "Sure was easier to do stuff in here than in my new truck."

I swallow hard. "Why did they do away with bench seats? Consoles just get in the way of...." Jeez, I'm getting lightheaded. "You know."

He nods. "I know." Then he smiles, and whoa.... "Good thing that you're not ovulating anymore. This old truck's safe tonight."

"What?" My pulse is pounding in my ears.

The cars ahead of us move again.

He doesn't answer.

I shift closer to him. "Why do you say it like that?"

"Come on, Roar. We've hooked up exactly once a month since August, except for two months where you managed to resist the urge."

"Well, I mean, like once a month was when the craving was the strongest, so to speak. It's not that I don't... It's not that you aren't... Are you fishing for compliments? Because I've already told you that you're very good looking. Extra good looking now, in fact. I don't know what you did with my boyfriend, but you've replaced him with like—"

I run out of words.

Garrett just stares at me.

"This is like when a comedian gets tapped to be like in the Marvel Cinematic Universe, and then they get jacked." Now I'm rambling. "You did that."

"I'm not that different."

"No, you were always hot." I laugh and grab for my hot chocolate, hiding behind the paper cup. "We shouldn't be talking about this."

His eyebrows curve up. "Why not? It's nicer than fighting. Come on, tell me more about how I was hot when I was a skinny high school kid."

He was skinny back in the day. A veritable beanpole, but he'd always been strong. Wiry. I take a sip of my drink and think about the advantages of him being whip-lean. "It made it very easy to straddle you on this bench seat, that's for sure."

He laughs out loud. "Oh, my God, don't get me thinking about that."

Now I'm giggling, too. "We're stuck in traffic. We don't have anything else to think about."

He moves the truck forward another six feet, then grabs his drink and adjusts himself on the driver's seat. It might be my imagination, but he flexes his thighs like he needs to create more room for his cock, which is...whew. I like that too much.

He clears his throat. "We could literally think about anything else. How about your aunt and your...nephews?"

"Cousins?" I dissolve into uncontrolled laughter. "You forgot the word cousins."

"I'm *distracted*. But yeah, let's, uh, talk about those rapscallions. How old are they now?"

"Three."

"Three. Great, they're going to be up *early* on Christmas morning." He glances sideways. "Are you ready to wake up early, since you agreed that we could sleep on the couches tomorrow night?"

"It seemed like a reasonable ask," I mutter, slightly annoyed that he's changed the subject away from flirting. Not that I *want* to flirt with him, exactly, but it was fun. "But is this really what you want to think about right now?"

Silence.

Then a groan, and that beautiful sound is the permission I need to say something truly reckless.

"Or would you rather think about how you taught me to grind on your thigh in this tru—"

"Come on."

"Okay, okay, I'm sorry." But I'm not. I'm turned on and aching.

"Two can play at that game." He gives me a hooded glare. "I mean, if we're going to think about memories that we made in this truck, we should get it right. I didn't teach you anything. We taught each other, maybe. Like when you wanted to jerk me off, but we didn't know what to do with the mess, so you just brought me to the edge over and over again, and then we stopped, and I went home and looked up if that was a thing because it was hot and then it turned out it was called edging, and you thought that was the funniest thing ever."

"Oh my God," I whisper. "I'd forgotten about that. That was…"

I trail off, a pang of longing shooting through my core. Because I can't say what I'm thinking.

That was amazing. And so out of reach for us now.

He takes a big gulp of hot chocolate and exhales. "Yeah."

"We had a lot of good times in this truck." I fan myself as the traffic in front of us suddenly eases. The moment is broken, and Garrett has to focus on driving again, because people are walking into the road all over the place.

I focus on the lit-up houses on my side of the road.

My sister's home is just ahead, and it's the only one not lit up like something right out of a Christmas movie. The pang in my chest twists into concern, and I file that away for later.

Jake and Dani's house is set further back from the road, down a long lane decorated with candy canes. Solar lights dot a separate pathway "to Santa's workshop", and people stream up and down it, but the lane itself is clear for our truck to pull up in front of the open garage.

Jake crosses to greet us with a big grin, a handshake for Garrett, and a warm hug for me. "Did you guys get roped into delivery duty right after arriving, or what?"

"We got fed dinner first, it's all good." Garrett gestures to the back of the truck. "You having a Christmas tree emergency?"

Jake laughs. But then his face turns serious, and he

makes careful eye contact with me. "Full disclosure, I think Dani was hoping Cassie would deliver them."

My heart thumps against my ribs. "Is Nate here?"

He shakes his head. "No. *No.* She wouldn't do that. She just wanted to see Cassie, but with all of this, she couldn't get away to come over to the farm. Nate's, uh, taken off for the holidays."

"What?"

He raises his hands. "Don't shoot the messenger. He left after they fought. So if Cassie wants to come home..."

"And be alone?" I cross my arms over my chest. "I don't think so. She's staying at the farm."

"Okay, okay."

His wife comes flying out of the house, a baby in a fleece bunting suit on her hip. "I'm so sorry I was inside. Hi Garrett," she adds breathlessly before enveloping me in a tight hug. "So good to see you, Rory. How was the drive?"

"Fine, but a shock to arrive to a crying sister. What do you know?"

"Not much." Dani passes her child to Jake. "Come on, I'll help with the trees and we can talk."

She takes one of the trees from the truck bed. I put one on my shoulder, and Garrett grabs the last two. We circle away from the light and noise at the front of the house, to her back deck. She has four tree stands waiting.

"So this wasn't a complete ruse to get my sister to come back?" I ask.

Dani winces. "No, of course not. This is a secret, but I'm pregnant again. This is how we're going to tell our families tomorrow."

"Oh my *Gosh*, Dani!" I jump up and down, so excited for her. "That's amazing news. How far along are you?"

"Twelve weeks. It's a little unexpected." Her cheeks

turn pink. "We spaced the first three kids out much better than this."

"It'll be all right," I promise her. "I'm so happy to be in on the secret!"

"You can tell your parents," she says. "How are they?"

"They're good. Busy with the farm, you know. How are yours?"

"Enjoying retirement." She rolls her eyes. "I wish we could make them talk."

I groan. "I know."

Then a child comes running, looking for his mom.

"I thought we could talk more," she says apologetically. "Are we doing diner lunch on the 26th?"

When I started my residency, and the Christmas break got squished down to a few days, we started carving out a dedicated Cousin Lunch where most of the Minelli cousins and the Kincaid cousins all descend on Mac's Diner—sans parents who don't speak to each other. And also without kids. "Of course we are. I'll make sure Cassie is there, too. See you in a couple days!"

Garrett says his congratulations to Dani as she's dragged away, then we're alone in her backyard.

"Wow, four kids," he says under his breath. Then he rubs his jaw and gestures. "Let's get back, I guess."

Regret slices through me. Followed by deep, frustrated jealousy that at some point, Garrett's going to meet a girl who wants to pop out baby after baby for him.

It's not that I don't want kids. I do. Theoretically, in the future. I've always wanted them...later. And now I'm thirty years old and my cousin who is only five years older than me has her *fourth* on the way and I'm eight months out of a breakup with the only guy I could imagine spawning the next generation of neurotic Minelli girls with. Or Minelli-

Kincaid girls. Or just Kincaid girls, because they don't have enough girls on that side of the family, and my mom's side is nothing but girls all the way back, so I'd probably—

"Hang on." Garrett catches me by the arm, spinning me around just before I reach the front of the house and all the lit up displays and the busybody neighbours checking it out.

All the breath whooshes out of me as I collide with his hard chest.

He wraps one of his arms around my back, bending me into the glow of the Christmas lights as he gently plucks at my hair with his free hand. "You've got some pine needles...here."

I stare up at him.

Even through our winter coats, I can feel the steel of his muscles banding around me, holding me tight.

He's letting his usually close-cropped beard thicken, like he always has over the holidays, and his blue-green eyes are glittering with intense focus as he de-Christmases my hair.

I'm sorry, I want to say, but the words don't come out. This isn't the time or the place.

"There you go," he murmurs.

Then his gaze flicks to meet mine. Heat flares low in my belly. A different kind of awareness than our dirty talk in the truck. This is way more dangerous. His eyes darken, his brows furrowing into a frown, but the moment doesn't break, it only intensifies. And there's a flare of something that makes me lightheaded. Slowly, his attention slides from my eyes to my mouth.

His hand slides out of my hair and along my jaw.

His thumb brushes at the corner of my mouth, then drops to catch me under the chin, holding my face up, as if he's afraid I'll look away and break this connection.

I should.

But I don't want to.

I really, really don't want to.

"Garrett," I whisper.

He leans in, curving into the embrace. But just as I think he's going to drop his mouth down onto mine, as I'm pressing up onto my toes inside my winter boots, there's laughter very close by.

"Oh, sorry," someone says, laughing as they bump into Garrett, a small crowd spilling around the corner of the house, intruding on our stolen private moment.

He turns us so I'm protected from the press of people, but he lets go of me at the same time.

By the time we make our way around them and wave goodbye to Jake and Dani in the garage-turned-Santa's workshop, Garrett's not looking at me and the almost kiss feels almost-imagined.

Chapter 10

Garrett

By the time we get back to the farm, the tree lot lights are off.

Rory leaps from the truck as soon as I come to a stop. I let her race ahead down the path.

After closing the gate, I put the keys to the truck in the sales hut, then instead of following her to the house, I shove my hands into my pockets and walk deeper into the tree lot, toward the skating trail.

There's a big moon tonight, so even though the lights are off, that's enough for me to help myself to a pair of rental skates in my size.

I hang up my coat on a hook and lace them on nice and tight.

I'm furious with myself for getting caught up in all of that with Rory. I want to be furious with her for starting the teasing in the truck, but I liked it too much. And it's not as if it's a secret that we still have wild chemistry.

Of course we do. We learned about sex together. There's nothing we can't say to each other—about sex.

But the embrace in the shadows of her cousin's house wasn't about sex.

That was all about the clawing need inside me to hold on to a woman I've already lost. Regret and what-ifs won't change that fact.

I used the excuse of her hair being covered in pine needles from the tree she carried to grab her as she raced away from me, the way she always races away when the topic of kids and marriage comes up. Not because I have any right to demand that she stop and tell me when she gave up that dream—it doesn't matter now—but because I wish I'd pinned her down on it years ago.

I wish we'd been able to talk about *that* a lot more. With the deep, raw, intimate honesty we can talk about edging.

Fuck my life.

I pump my legs, taking the first curve into the forest with some speed. The skates bite on the freshly sprayed ice. I built Dante a mini homemade Zamboni a few years ago, the second year they had this skating trail, and it makes easy work of the nightly maintenance.

Has Rory noticed that I'm not behind her? Has her family asked her why she's returned alone? What has she told them?

What would she have told them if that shitbox hatchback had worked long enough to get her here?

Was I that easily erased from her life?

This is the only immediate family I have now. My mom left when I was a baby. My dad did his best, with a lot of community help, but by the time I was in school, I was pretty much on my own. His death two years ago only made official an orphan status I think I've always felt in my bones. There was never a lunch that I didn't pack myself—until the end of high school, when I started crashing on Rory's couch some nights, just to not be alone.

Carmen always packed me a lunch in the morning.

All of that history just wiped away because I wanted too much from Rory.

Fucking hell.

The next curve in the trail leads into a fun little chunk of twists and turns. A clever way to create more skating distance in a limited footprint. I take it as fast as safely possible, then hit the last straightaway with a good amount of speed.

The last person I'm expecting to see when I hit the open part of the trail near the skate shack is Rory.

She raises her hand in silent greeting, then steps onto the ice.

She's borrowed skates, too. But she's family. She's allowed.

"I thought you went up to the house," I manage to say as I slow down.

She spins and starts skating backward so she's looking at me. "I got halfway there when I heard you through the trees. I might not get a chance to skate tomorrow, so... Can I join you?"

I grunt. "You already did."

"Do you want to race?" She twists around, her little legs powering up.

Rory's a good skater, and she's built for speed, with thick thighs for her little build, and a nice low centre of gravity.

But my legs are twice as long as hers, and I'm already warmed up.

Also, I'm not feeling charitable at the moment.

No, I don't want to race. I want to chase her deep into

the forest and then fuck her against a tree.

Since I can't do that, I shoot past her and take off, letting her chase me for once.

She keeps up pretty well. I stretch out the lead only to lose it on the twists and turns. As we shoot past the skate hut on the next pass, I can hear that she's still with me.

Can't shake her, so I slow down.

She comes alongside me but doesn't try to initiate a conversation again. We skate three more laps together, until she's breathing hard. When she pulls off, I follow, even though I could have kept going for a while.

Silently, we take care of the skates.

Then we put our coats back on and walk back to the house together.

Just before we get to the porch, she grabs my arm.

"Hey, um…" She rolls her head and puffs a long breath up into the night sky.

But before she can finish her thought, the door swings open and Cassie waves a bottle of wine at us. "What took you guys so long? I'm getting Mom drunk, get in here."

"Oh, brother," Rory mutters under her breath.

"We'll talk later," I promise her, anxiety twisting low in my gut. I don't really want to talk. It never goes well. But there are things left unsaid between us, and tonight might be the last time we ever get to be truly alone.

I'm not going to waste that opportunity.

"Come on," Cassie wheedles as Rory firmly sets an empty bottle of wine—the second one we've put away—in the recycling bin. "You make the best shots, just do one special Christmas one for us."

"Nope. Not doing shots tonight. We have an early morning."

Carmen wraps her arms around Cassie from behind and gives Rory a pouting face. I think she may have had more wine than either of her daughters.

I glance at Dante, who has been nursing the same glass of whiskey all night. He shakes his head.

"I know better than to get involved," he mutters. "I'm off to bed."

He kisses Carmen, reminds his daughters that they have a big day tomorrow, and then he escapes.

I should do the same.

But I also need to hang around in case Rory needs to be rescued.

"Fine," she relents. "One round."

She crosses to the big hutch that serves as the Minelli liquor cabinet. Tapping her lower lip in a very distracting way, she considers her options. "Chocolate? Mint?"

"Yes," Cassie says firmly. "Two rounds of shots."

"Or we combine them." Rory winks and plunks a bottle of white chocolate liqueur in front of where I'm sprawled at the big kitchen table. "Hold this."

I hold it.

She digs out peppermint schnapps and vanilla vodka.

Then a shaker.

"We're getting serious now," Carmen giggles, leaning on the table.

"One shot," I remind everyone.

But then Rory puts a lot of ice in the shaker, and she free pours way more than three shots worth of the different ingredients.

"Oops," she says. "Oh well."

She shakes it up like a pro, then grabs four shot glasses. "You in, Garrett?"

"Yeah, sure."

She pours them up and we lean in, tapping our shots together before swallowing the delicious but deadly combination that tastes just like peppermint bark candy.

"Now it feels like Christmas," Cassie says, wiping her mouth.

Rory and I exchange a look. We're both thinking the same thing. She lives—lived?—across the road from Santa's Workshop on the Polar Expressway, and *this* is what pushes her into Christmas vibes?

"One more," Rory says, urging us all to put our glasses in again.

I push out of my chair and shake my head. "I'm good."

I cross to the sink to wash my shot glass as they do another round.

Carmen sighs happily. "I should follow your dad to bed. Night night, my babies."

I hold my breath until she's out of the room.

Rory and her mom have an interesting relationship. They love each other fiercely, but they also butt heads constantly, and it feels like a miracle that they didn't argue tonight—and that Carmen didn't find a way to blame Rory for Cassie's breakup, as she feared.

Now that she's heading upstairs, I should do the same.

"Can I trust you two to close this place down by yourselves?" I ask, going for lighthearted.

Rory nods, not quite meeting my gaze.

But Cassie protests. "No, stay up with us."

For good measure, she pouts, a mirror of her mother.

Rory rolls her eyes. "You just want a chaperone so I

don't ask you about Nate, but Garrett won't stop me from doing that, so put that manipulative lip away."

"Ouch." Cassie snatches at the shaker. "Let's make more drinks."

"Nope."

But Cassie doesn't need Rory to play bartender. She was watching the first time, and now she freehands her own version of the peppermint bark shot over the remaining ice in the shaker.

Rory peels off her sweater, leaving her in just a cotton tank top that's wrinkled from her body heat and slipping off her shoulder.

I stare at her bra strap and think about sliding my finger under it and dragging her off to bed.

Maybe that shot was a bad idea.

Maybe a second shot would be a good idea.

"Maybe you should tell us what happened," Rory says.

Right.

Cassie. We need to focus on Cassie.

Rory's sister puffs out her cheeks. "I'm too much for him."

Oh shit. No, I shouldn't be here for this.

Rory goes still. "What the hell does that mean?"

Cassie waves her hands in the air. "You know. You say it too. I'm a lot."

"Yeah, but you've always been a lot, and it's...loveable."

"Well, it's more loveable when you're an eager twenty-one-year-old, I guess." Cassie's lower lip wobbles and her eyes start to swim with tears.

"He didn't fucking say that, did he?" I hear myself growl that out. I didn't have *track down my brother-in-law and wrestle him down to the ground for being an asshole* on my Christmas bingo card, but we'll do what we need to do.

She shakes her head. "Not exactly. But he always used to say I was his wild girl or his..." She hiccups. "His feral monster."

"You're hardly feral," Rory mutters. "That's more Jules territory."

I stretch my leg under the table and nudge her chair.

She swings her head my way, her eyes slow to focus on my face. "What? Why'd you nudge me?"

I cover my face as my shoulders shake with laughter.

"What???" Rory sounds so confused. Adorably, drunkenly confused.

"He doesn't mean feral like Jules," I mumble from behind my hands. "Not like a selfish little goblin. More... uninhibited."

Rory's mouth falls open. "Oh." Her eyes go wide. "*Oh.* Is this about s-e-x?"

Cassie makes a face. "Don't be immature."

"I'm not *immature* about sex. I'm just seeking *clarity* and trying to do it *delicately*."

I push to my feet. "This conversation might be easier if I'm not here. I'm going to take a shower."

And because I'm supposed to be her boyfriend, I go around the table and squeeze Rory's tense shoulder. A pretence of saying goodnight, but really trying to convey to her that she was never too much, no matter what she thinks.

But because I'm no longer her boyfriend, it doesn't help.

I'm just pulling a t-shirt over my damp-from-the-shower hair when Rory tumbles into the room we're sharing tonight.

"Oops," she says, her gaze snagging on my bare abdomen before I smooth the cotton over it. "Sorry."

"No worries."

She flops on the bed. "Need to set my alarm."

"Where's your phone?"

"Dunno."

I catch her leg and roll her onto her side. "In your back pocket."

She gasps. "Thank you."

After she mashes her fingers against the screen, she shoves her phone in my general direction.

I take it and put it on the bedside table. "Can I recommend something comfortable to sleep in? Maybe brush your teeth, too?"

"Yeah, I should. I will." She gets up and stumbles out into the hallway.

"I'll get your PJs," I say at her retreating back.

She's already unpacked, so I go to the dresser and pull open the top drawer. There are two sets of over-the-top Christmas sleep wear—right next to my green flannel shirt, carefully folded.

Interesting.

Maybe she's going to give it to me for Christmas.

Maybe she'll keep it forever.

I grab the softer, more worn PJs, a red cotton set covered in oversized lights.

She comes back, already pulling off her clothes.

I've always loved how much of a nudist Rory can be, but given that she's drunk and she's never liked fooling around in her parents' house while they're home, I stop her when she gets down to her tank top and her panties.

"Here you go," I say, kneeling in front of her. "Put these on."

She puts her hands on my shoulders as she steps into the pants. "You don't need to take care of me."

"I know."

"But you are."

"Bare minimum." I tug the waistband up her thighs, ignoring the way her skin feels as my thumbs graze her body. "A peace offering, if you will."

"Two in one day, we're maturing."

I push to my feet and hold up the top. "Do you want to wear this, too?"

She makes a face. "Too hot."

"K. Turn around."

"Why?"

"Are you going to take off your own bra?"

She contorts her arms, the huffs a frustrated breath and spins dangerously.

I catch her by the shoulders. "Let me."

She shivers as I lift her tank top up and slide my hands under it, expertly finding the clasp and releasing her tits from their confine.

"Thanks," she whispers as she pulls away. She hangs the bra on one of the dresser knobs, then climbs into bed.

I follow, my pulse heavy, my cock ignoring my brain's blaring reminder that this isn't like *that*.

She stretches out on her side, and I roll onto my back. My arm comes up, muscle memory getting it halfway across her pillow before I remember that we aren't going to snuggle all night.

I don't stop soon enough for her not to notice, and she tugs her pillow all the way to the edge of the bed.

I sigh. "I'll stay on my own side."

She flops onto her back, cheeks flushed, and crosses her

arms tightly in front of her. She's defiant and gorgeous in her drunken indignation. "I didn't say anything."

"You didn't need to. I'll keep my hands to myself, too."

She doesn't reply to that.

Which is...curious.

So I add, "Unless you text me in the middle of the night."

Her mouth opens. Closes.

"Not happening," she mutters, turning over to give me her back.

I'm grinning as she turns off the lamp, plunging the room into darkness.

Feeling her settle next to me after all these months is interesting. Of course I know what it's like to have her close, to hold her tightly. Did that just three days ago, after all. But none of our hookups were in a bed. And I didn't think we'd get to actually *sleep* together again, let alone in *this* bed.

Tension radiates off her tight little body.

But we survived eight hours in the truck, and hours with her family. We can handle a night sharing a room.

Chapter 11

Rory

Garrett's breathing slows and evens out.

It should be soothing.

Instead, it's exactly the right bass line rhythm for my brain to parade out all of my choices today, in a reverse march of *what the fuck were you thinking, Rory Minelli?*

From the way he kept watching me in the kitchen as we did those shots, to the Christmas tree delivery, to me calling him *babe* as soon as I realized we couldn't tell my family we'd broken up, to the long drive, all the way back to his arrival in the parking lot behind my apartment.

The weird relief I felt, even as resentment made me prickly. It's not his fault that I ignored the warning lights on the car.

I drag in a slow, long breath, but that just pulls in the scent of his soap rising off his warm, sleeping body. Makes my thoughts spiral from the parade of regrets to more chaotic, clashing visuals. Sex and kissing and not kissing and babies and work and being too much and not enough.

The way I automatically asked him for help.

And how he instinctively stepped up.

How it's been hours and we haven't fought.

We've almost kissed and we've raced around the skating trail and we made questionable choices about drinking the night before a very busy Christmas Eve. But we also busted his ninety minute rule wide open.

I *hate* that we got to a place where he had to put a time limit on being around me.

Also on my hate list is the fact my sister is struggling, too, like we're both—

"Roar?"

I hold my breath.

"I know you're awake." His voice is low, but it wraps around me, squeezing every inch of my skin in the dark.

"I'm fine," I whisper automatically. "I just can't sleep."

"You want to talk about anything?"

I swallow around all of my spinning thoughts. "You were really helpful tonight."

"That's keeping you up?"

That's the thin edge of the wedge, but I don't want to talk about the rest of it. "I don't really deserve that kindness. But I do appreciate it."

He exhales. "You do deserve it, though. That's the thing."

I screw up my face and don't say anything.

"Do you want to talk about Cassie?" he asks after a minute of pregnant silence.

"No."

"Do you want to talk about us?"

"There is no us." God, my voice sounds small. I meant it as an objective fact, but Garrett picks up on the hurt that's too hard to hide.

"I know." He sighs. "You tensed up when Cassie said

Nate thinks she's a lot. And I just wanted to say that I don't think you're too much. You're...great."

"That would be more believable if you didn't hesitate before saying great."

"It's not hesitation. It's uncertainty about how far I should go in praising my stubborn ex while we're sharing a blanket."

"You don't need to praise me at all. I know I've dragged you into a big family mess, and I'm sorry about that."

"It's my family mess, too." His voice turns rough.

I turn my head sideways.

Even in the dark, I can tell that he's looking at me.

And now I can't look away.

"That's why I went skating tonight," he adds. "I, uh, thought it might be my last time on the trail alone. And I was thinking about how your family is my only family, too. I know, I have my cousins, but *this* is where I come home for Christmas. You don't need to feel bad about dragging me into anything, Roar. I invited myself because I didn't have anywhere else to go. And I didn't know that last year was my last year in this family, so having a redo on that—"

"You're always going to be welcome here." The words are tight, but it's not hard to say, because it's the truth. "My parents love you. And who knows, maybe *I* won't come home for Christmas next year. You can have them all to yourself."

"Why do you say that?"

"I don't even know where I'll be. But, uh, it probably won't be Ottawa." It's a confession a long time coming. My head spins at the relief of finally admitting the truth.

"You're moving? What happened to getting hired on at the hospital?" When I don't answer, he sighs again. "You don't have to tell me if you don't want to."

"It's not you. I don't want to talk about it at all." I inhale slowly. "What about you? Are you going to stay in Ottawa?"

"Haven't thought about it." He rolls onto his back, staring up at the ceiling. Not looking at me anymore, his body language clearly projecting that he needs a second to process what I've just said. "Where else are you looking?"

"I'm not yet. I know I should. By the time I do, I'll probably only have leftover remote job opportunities."

"Jesus, Rory."

"I know."

He doesn't need to say anything else. I know he doesn't have a lot of respect for the training program that has chewed me up, and he doesn't understand my stubbornness about my career path. It's hard to explain even to myself, which is why I'm stuck in this spot.

"You can't use me for sex to avoid life," he finally says.

I choke on a sad laugh. "Yeah, I know. Which is a real shame, because whew, that works like nothing else."

"Yeah?" He turns his head.

It feels good to have him looking at me again.

I nod. "It's like horny arguing flips a switch that shuts my brain up."

He makes a sound that could be a laugh or a groan. "That checks out."

Then he shifts, the mattress dipping between us, and I feel the pull. It would be easy to roll into him.

Pick a fight as he gathers me in his arms, as he tugs my hair and guides my mouth anywhere but his. He'd let me bite him sooner than kiss him.

We could exhaust ourselves with fucking and go to sleep in a messy tangle.

But we'd wake up tomorrow in exactly the same place—

Garrett not happy because I'm not happy, and me... confused. Unable to find my way out of the tangle.

"I don't want that anymore."

Silence.

Then...

"Okay," he says, like it's easy.

That hurts. But I did it to myself.

"I liked that we didn't fight tonight," I whisper after a long quiet.

"Me, too." His hand is still between us, but he turns it and grips the edge of his pillow. "It felt like we were on the same side."

It really did. "We should do that more often. Maybe try being friends."

"Roar," he says, and I hear the smile in it, but I also feel the ache. "We've always been friends."

I slide my hand out from the covers.

I shouldn't hook my pinky finger through his, the only one not tightly wound around the edge of his pillow. That's blurring the line of tentative friendship, I'm sure.

I do it anyway.

It's ridiculous how much my body unclenches at such a tiny point of contact. He's always been an anchor, and I've been using him for months.

The darkness of the room, the lateness of the night, slowly settles around us.

"I'm going to try to be a good friend," I say, the promise more to myself than to him.

"Same." Through the dim, I see the corner of his mouth quirk up. "First friend up in the morning makes coffee?"

"Deal."

"Both of our phones are on my side of the bed," he

points out. "Unless you've got your pager secreted away somewhere, you aren't waking up first."

"I promise, the pager is in my backpack and turned off. But if you want me to sleep with my phone under my pillow..."

He reaches for it, and our pinkies tug, but neither of us lets go. He passes it to me, and I check the alarm is set.

"Fair is fair," I whisper as I tuck it under my head.

He squeezes my finger with his.

"Night, Roar," he says.

And the urge to cross the small gap between us, to plant my mouth against his, is nearly overwhelming. Nostalgia and familiarity are potent traps.

It's good that we're only sleeping in this bed tonight. Tomorrow, we'll safely be on opposite couches.

I swallow and make a silent pledge. I won't kiss him. Not tonight. Not tomorrow. I'm going to protect the fragile thing we're building, brick by careful brick. "Good night."

This time when I listen to his breathing even out, I don't make the mistake of thinking he's asleep. I know he's not. I'm not alone in having heavy thoughts swirling.

But I can also feel his pulse, faint and steady, through our hooked fingers. I count the rhythm, and slowly, my pulse slows down to match his. My breathing, too, and finally, blissfully, my thoughts start to fragment in that pre-sleep way.

Kissing. Not kissing. Christmas vibes. Stern looks. Confusing looks. Finding Garrett through the chaos.

Tomorrow *is* going to be chaos.

It'll be chaos with Garrett at the centre of it, though, and that's something to look forward to.

Chapter 12

Rory

I wake up alone, sprawled in the middle of the bed. Garrett apparently got my phone out from under my pillow and silenced my alarm without me noticing.

Heart pounding, I roll back onto my own side and flop back against the pillows.

There's a quiet knock at the door, then it swings open.

As soon as Garrett steps inside, the whole conversation from last night floods back to me.

"Hi," I say, pushing myself up, feeling flushed and oddly out of sorts.

Friends. We're going to really try to be friends here.

His gaze drops to my tank top for a second.

Do friends stare at each other's tits? We need to do some work there. But I let him take my bra off, so...

He holds out a mug. "Good morning."

"Thank you." I take it and bring it to my mouth, inhaling the faint cinnamon that's the hallmark of my dad's Christmas Eve morning coffee. "Is everyone up?"

"Yep. Our alarms didn't even go off. I woke up to your mom and Cassie arguing right outside your door."

I wince. "Wow, I slept through that?"

"You were zonked. I would have let you sleep more, but pancakes and sausages are almost ready."

"It's okay, I woke up on my own. What were they fighting about?"

He shrugs. "Doesn't matter."

"That means it was some variation of *Why don't you talk to your sister more?* Which is the first step to making Cassie's breakup my fault for not being a mind reader."

Garrett toasts me with his own mug. "But you clearly are a mind reader, because that's bang on."

I growl under my breath.

He waves it off. "It doesn't matter, because Jules is here."

"What?" I scramble off the bed, my coffee sloshing dangerously.

Garrett catches the mug deftly. "It's chilly downstairs, if you want to put on another layer."

I glance down at my thin tank top. "Good point."

He nods to the dresser. "Your matching PJ top is in the top drawer. Right next to my green flannel shirt."

Ah, crap.

"Busted," I say lightly.

"So you didn't bring it to return it?"

"After all these months, I think it's mine now." I yank the drawer open and grab it. "In fact, I'm going to wear it now. Possession is nine tenths of the law."

"So you're staking a claim."

"I'm the one who brought it here."

"I'm just saying."

I shove my arms into the shirt. It's warm and cozy and way too big for me. "I don't understand. What *are* you saying?"

Garrett hands me my coffee back as I stalk to the door.

But he doesn't get out of the way.

He tugs at the loose edge of the shirt, then adjusts the collar, his fingers so close to my neck I can feel the heat of his hand even though he doesn't actually touch my skin.

"Pretty sure you go storming downstairs in my shirt, your cheeks all pink like that, your family is going to think I came up here, kissed you awake, then put my shirt on you, like *I'm* the one staking a claim." He pauses. "But I guess that's what we want them to think right now, isn't it?"

"Um," I managed to say, which isn't saying anything at all. "Yes?"

And it comes out like a question.

"We haven't talked about how this plan plays out." His gaze searches my face, his eyes carefully guarded.

I swallow hard. "I know."

"Rory!" my baby sister calls from downstairs. "Where is Mini Minelli?"

"I'm coming," I yell back. Then I take a big, fortifying sip of coffee. "Thank you for this. It's perfect. You're perfect. I'll figure out a graceful exit plan at some point today."

He puts his arm across the door, stopping me from ducking around him. "We."

"What?"

"*We* will figure out a plan." His jaw clenches, his mouth pulling tight, before his gaze softens in exasperation. "You keep too much to yourself, Roar. If we're friends, we're in this together. And we don't need an exit plan just yet. Let's focus on having a good Christmas first."

If we're friends. There's a lot riding on that *if.*

The doorknob rattles, and he steps out of the way as

Jules explodes into the room. The youngest sister is also the tallest, and she has to lean over to hug me.

"Mini," she says happily. "You're finally awake."

"Where the heck did you come from, Baby?"

"I drove up last night."

"After *working* last night," Cassie adds, barging in. "She got in at three in the morning!"

"Jules," I admonish.

She rolls her eyes. "I got here safely, didn't I? Besides, Cassie is in crisis."

Garrett clears his throat. "I'll go help your dad with breakfast."

Once he's gone, I cup my little sister's pretty, concerned face. "Cassie's doing okay."

"Tell that to Mom," our middle sister mutters. "She was holding herself back last night. This morning she's more teary than I am."

"Seriously, Mini, you need to come downstairs." Jules pulls Cassie into our hug. "Mom doesn't understand that once a man dumps a Minelli girl, he's dead to us."

I wince. "Um—"

"And this one is better off without that loser."

"He's not a loser," Cassie protests.

That remains to be seen, but given my own circumstances, I have to give Nate the benefit of the doubt here. I focus on Jules. "What did she tell you?"

"Who, Mom?"

"No, Cassie!"

"I'm right here," our sister says.

"I know, Middle, but you both plowed into here like there was something urgent that I needed to sort out, so I'm guessing something new has spilled out since last night?" I look back and forth between them. "Yes? No?"

Jules shakes her head. "She didn't give me anything. All I know from Mom is that Cassie showed up here crying and Nate is MIA."

I rub my temple. "Cassie, you don't know where he went? Did you try texting him?"

She crosses her arms over her chest. "I blocked his number."

"Great. Real mature."

"Girls!" Mom interrupts us from downstairs. "Breakfast!"

"Okay, here's what we're going to do." I take both of their hands. "For the morning, nothing matters other than selling Christmas trees. And then as soon as we sell the last tree, we're hopping on the wagon into town, and we're going to buy the most obscene Christmas treats for tonight at the market. We aren't going to talk about relationships, or men, *all day*. Got it? If Mom tries to bring it up, just say *that doesn't pass the Bechdel Test* and change the subject back to trees."

"She's not going to know what that is," Cassie says.

"*I* don't know what that is," Jules adds.

"*What?*" Cassie and I say at the same time.

She shrugs, unbothered.

"We've failed you," Cassie says dramatically.

"It's basically a measure of a story revolving around a man," I say. "Do two or more female characters have a conversation about something that isn't about a male character?"

"Do fictional men with wings or horns count? Because that's exclusively what I'm consuming right now."

"It's not a criticism of what you're reading, Baby. I don't remember the last time I read for pleasure at all. Wings and horns sound amazing, even attached to men. But *right now*, today, we're going to use it to our advantage with Mom. We are more than the sum of our relationships, and on one of our favourite days of the year, we aren't going to focus on menfolk."

Cassie pumps her fist. "Amen."

I push her out the door. "Let's go eat. We have trees to sell."

Jules ruffles my hair. Despite probably getting only three hours sleep, her longer hair looks great. Sleek dark-brown waves spill over her slim shoulders. In comparison, my frizzy shoulder-length bob probably looks frightening, but that's a problem for after breakfast.

"How are you?" she asks as we follow Cassie down the stairs. "Are you sleeping? You don't look like you're sleeping."

"I slept great last night," I say, and it's not even a lie.

"Sleep is the most important health factor that we have complete control over," she says with all the confidence of a twenty-two year old.

"Tell that to the labouring moms in L&D," I say lightly, because she's not wrong. Sleep *is* important. It's just not something that residents get to do.

I'll sleep when I'm a consultant. Or maybe when I'm retired.

She makes a worrying sound. "I know how hard it is to get up in the middle of the night."

"Okay." I stop at the bottom of the stairs and pin a glare on her. "Getting up for a fussy two-year-old isn't the same as—"

"We don't need to dive right into comparisonitis," Cassie tries to intervene.

But Jules is already flaring for an indignant fight. "Are you saying my job isn't hard?"

"I didn't—"

"Do you know hard it is to work for elite talent?"

I roll my eyes.

That only fires her up more. "My job is just as important as yours!"

Garrett appears in the doorway of the kitchen, his broad shoulders a welcome distraction. "Who wants pancakes?"

I slide into the chair closest to where his coffee mug is, and as soon as he puts plates in front of my sisters, he joins me.

His knee bumps mine under the table. "I put extra sausages on your plate, but if you don't want them, I'll eat them."

"Thanks." I grab the carafe of coffee from the middle of the table and top up my mug, then offer it to him. "More coffee?"

He smiles and holds out his mug. "Now we're tied."

"For what?"

"Getting each other coffee."

"Oh!" I laugh. "I guess we are."

Jules coughs. "Mini, can you pass the coffee down here when you're done batting your eyes at Garrett?"

"Bechdel Test," Cassie mutters, like it's a safe word.

Garrett furrows his brows. "Pardon?"

I wave it off. "So how many trees do we need to sell today, Dad?"

My mom bustles in from the back room, holding a notepad. Her face is shiny from crying, but she's putting on a brave smile now. "Are you girls going to the market this afternoon?"

When my dad put in the skating trail, he got a permit from the town to run a horse-drawn wagon between the farm and Main Street on Christmas Eve. And the following year, some of the downtown retailers organized a Last Minute Christmas Market. When we sold out of trees, my dad gave us each some spending money and put us on the wagon to get treats for Christmas Eve.

A sister tradition was born.

"As long as they sell the remaining twenty-eight trees on the lot," my dad jokes.

"Oh, we're going to do that by lunch!" Jules declares with confidence.

"Do you want us to pick stuff up for tonight or tomorrow?" I ask. "Text me a list."

My mom tears a sheet out of the notebook and sets it next to my plate. "That would be a big help, thank you."

Garrett reaches across, grabs the handwritten page, and takes a picture. He taps on his phone screen. "I'll text it to you."

Mom beams at him. "You're so helpful, Garrett. Maybe you should have a talk with Nate—"

"Bechdel Test," Jules yells.

My mom looks at her, startled. "What do you mean?"

Jules gives me an expectant stare.

Right.

My idea, my explanation. "Mom, we want to focus on the holidays today. No more talking about men. And I asked you to text me a list. Garrett was just doing that for you, because you ignored me when *I* said it."

Her face pinches up. "Well, I'm sorry, I guess."

It's Christmas Eve, so we'll move past the qualifier. "Thank you. I love you."

"Of course, I love you, too. But I don't see how it's a bad thing to notice how helpful Garrett is. Anyway," she adds, blazing right past the passive aggressive guilting, "you're right that we should focus on the holidays when we only have you girls here for such a short amount of time."

"About that," Jules says, wincing. "I need to leave right after Cousin Lunch on Boxing Day."

"Okay," Garrett says, cutting off my mother's protest. "So we need to maximize every single second of Christmas Eve and Christmas Day, right? That's what we're all saying? Twenty-eight trees to sell. Where do you need me, Dante? Put me to work."

Chapter 13

Garrett

When we're upstairs in Rory's room, she flings my shirt onto the bed.

"Close your eyes," she says, which is ridiculous, because I've seen her naked on a daily basis for more than a decade.

Instead, I shut the door and lean back against it. "Bechdel Test?"

"It's like a safe word for mother daughter relations."

"Ah."

She peels off her PJ pants and digs out a pair of leggings. "What's the temperature today?"

"Just above freezing. Maybe two degrees?"

"These are fleece-lined, I think I'll be okay." She tugs them on, then glances back at me. "You didn't close your eyes."

"I can see you naked with my eyes closed, too. I've got a whole collection of Rory highlights." I snag the green flannel shirt off the bed. It smells like her, warm and sweet, so I pull it on over my t-shirt. "Reclaimed."

She rolls her eyes. "Are you ready to go over to the tree lot?"

"Yep."

"Then go." She crosses her arms over her tank top-clad chest. "I don't need an audience for putting on a bra and finding a sweater."

But the audience would really enjoy that. Except I can't tell her that. "All right, you win. See you out there."

By mid-morning, the tree farm is already packed with families. I'm lazily doing laps of the skating trail, which is cooler than the sunny lot, where the snow from yesterday has already melted. No white Christmas for Pine Harbour after all.

But on the trail, where the sun can't really break through the dense trees and the ice stays frozen, there's a certain Polar Whimsy in the air.

Kids are wearing oversized elf hats on their helmets and parents are dancing to songs that would be right at home on Rory's playlist.

A group of teenagers blows past me, laughing and showing off. I recognize a few of them. They're good kids, just excited about the holidays.

I round the first curve into the forest when I hear the distinctive sound of blades catching wrong, followed by an ominous thud, a body landing hard on the ice.

Panicked voices immediately follow. "Oh shit, oh shit!"

I pump my legs hard, shooting around the bend to find a teenage girl sprawled on the ice. Her friends are clustered around her, their faces all tight with fear.

Shit. Injuries are a fact of life, and skaters need to sign a waiver, but still. Fuck. Bad vibes on Christmas Eve.

I'm on the radio as I stop next to them. "This is Garrett at Turn One, standby for an incident report."

Then I drop to my knees beside her.

She's conscious, but looks dazed, blinking up at me with unfocused eyes.

"Hey there," I say gently. "What's your name?"

"Emma," she whispers.

"Hi, Emma. I'm Garrett. Don't try to move yet, okay? Can you tell me what hurts?"

"My arm." Tears leak from the corners of her eyes. "I can't move it without—*ow*."

My radio crackles. It's Rory. "*Roger. Standing by.*"

I smile reassuringly at Emma. "We're going to get you some help, then. Did you know that there's a doctor who moonlights here doing Christmas tree sales?"

She doesn't laugh, but her friends do.

"I'm serious." I look at her most anxious looking friend. Kids like him need a task in an emergency. Sure, I have the radio, but I might as well let him help. "Can you go backwards on the trail—you won't get in trouble, I promise—and meet Dr. Minelli there and show her where we are?"

He takes off like a shot.

As soon as he's out of sight, I hop on the radio again. "Roar, meet a kid at the skate hut. Bring the first aid kit. I think you'll need a sling."

I turn back to Emma. "You're going to be in very good hands soon. How many fingers am I holding up?"

"Three."

"Good. What day is it?"

"Christmas Eve." She tries to smile, then winces. "My mom's going to kill me."

"Is she here?"

"Yeah. She wanted to..." Emma sobs. "Surprise my dad with a real tree."

I get back on the radio and manage to relay to Cassie who we're looking for.

By the time that conversation is over, Rory's coming around the corner. She makes quick eye contact with me, then looks back at the kid skating along beside where she's walking at the edge of the trail. She's listening to him, but her sharp gaze is taking in the scene.

She's wearing the same Pine Harbour Little Tree Farm puffy vest that I am, over a fluffy cream sweater.

"Hi, Emma. I'm Rory. I understand you fell on your arm." Her voice is all business, cool and competent. She touches my shoulder as she kneels down, guiding me out of the way. "Does anything else hurt?"

After doing a quick check on Emma's head and legs, she glances around. "Let's move everyone out of the way a bit. Can someone go and find Emma's boots for me, please? Emma, I want to get you sitting up. Then we can slide your coat off and get your arm in a sling to go to the hospital." She shrugs out of her vest and lays it on the ground beside the ice. "I'm going to brace your arm against your body, and Garrett is going to help get you up, okay?"

Emma's eyes flare wide in alarm. "It hurts to move."

"Let's wait for your mom, then. We can cut your coat off if need be."

"No, don't..." Emma's face screws up, tears welling.

"Hey, it's okay." Rory lowers her voice, whispering to the girl, until her panic subsides. "That's it. Just keep breathing."

"Oh my God, Emma!" A woman comes running along the trail. "I'm her mother."

Rory introduces herself.

"I'm okay, Mom," Emma says, though she looks far from it.

Rory repeats the options about the coat, and explains that the arm will hurt less once it's in a sling. "And you know what? Once you get to the hospital and they get it in a cast, the pain will almost completely go away. Casts are literally magic. Science magic. So the sooner we can get you up, the sooner you'll feel better."

"I..." Emma looks up at us and starts crying again.

Rory patiently explains how she would brace the girl's arm, minimizing the movement as much as possible.

And finally, Emma agrees to let us lift her up to sitting.

Rory uses her own arm like a firm splint, and I put my arms behind Emma's shoulders and legs. On three, we lift her up and sit her on Rory's vest.

Silent tears spill down her face as I ease her coat off her uninjured arm first, then Rory slides it off her almost-definitely fractured forearm next.

"Garrett, can you hold her arm against her body just like this," Rory says. "I'll put a sling on you, Emma, and then we'll get your coat back on you, I know it's cold."

"I'm okay," the teenager says between tightly pinched lips.

"You're being so brave. Almost done." Rory ties off the fabric at Emma's neck, then deftly pulls her coat around her shoulders. "Let's get your skates off, and your boots on, and then you're going to very carefully walk out of here like a rockstar, with this big entourage around you to make sure you're safe."

Once she's up on her feet, between Rory and her mom, I go to the skate hut with her friends to return everyone's skates, and get my own boots on as well.

By the time I get to the tree lot, Emma is in the back of her mom's car.

"I'll call the hospital and let them know you're coming," Rory says. "Keep me posted. And I'll come sign your cast tomorrow if you're up for a visitor."

Then they pull away.

Emma's friends melt away, finding their families in the crowd.

"Well done, Dr. Minelli," I tease.

She rolls her eyes.

Except it *is* impressive to watch her work.

She walks away from the crowd as she searches for the hospital phone number.

I follow because I have nothing else to do at the moment, and I'm still carrying her puffy vest. Silently, I hold it up. *Do you want this back?*

She shakes her head. In the sun, it's quite warm now, and after that blast of excitement, I'm warm, too.

As she waits on hold to be transferred to the emergency department, I hang both of our vests up on a hook on the tree sales hut.

"How's business?" I ask Cassie.

"Jules is telling every customer that their aura is calling out for a very specific tree, so she's moving an average of two per household."

Her sister jogs over. "Just sold four more."

"Auras?" I ask.

She grins wickedly. "Yep."

"You're evil."

"This is business," she says with savage delight. "And also, I'm hungry and want to go to the bakery."

"Yeah, I think we'll be sold out within the hour," Cassie says dryly.

I give them both a high five, then go to give the good news to Rory.

"That's right," she says into the phone as I approach. "Briefly dazed but is now alert and well-oriented. Possible concussion, but her helmet was on properly. Yep, sounds good. Thanks."

"All good?" I ask after she ends the call.

"Yep."

"Your sisters seem to have the tree sales under control."

"Mm-hmm." Rory glances around. "Are you heading back to the skating trail?"

"I think they're okay without me. You want to get a hot chocolate?"

She shakes her head, then flicks her gaze over the tree lot.

"Do you want to walk the lines and do a tree count?" I guess.

Her cheeks turn pink. "How did you guess?"

"It's Christmas Eve. You and your dad are both creatures of habit."

"Are we?" She looks genuinely delighted at that. "That's a very nice way to say dogmatically hyper focused."

"That's a very critical way to say creature of habit."

"Touché." She starts counting, and it doesn't take long. "Eight! We only have eight trees left!"

I'm laughing as she jumps up and down in excitement.

And then suddenly she's right in front of me, and it's the most natural thing in the world to catch her in my arms and twirl her around.

When I set her down, my arms stay around her and her hands stay on my chest.

"This is exciting," I manage to say.

She nods, her eyes bright. "Yeah. I should go tell my sisters."

But neither of us moves.

The air around us might be hovering just above freezing, but with Rory's body pressed against mine, it feels like I'm on fire.

"I want you to have a good Christmas," I say thickly.

"I am. And you, too. I want—" She clenches her fist around the flannel shirt I'm wear. That she was wearing. That I've fucked her in, and covered her naked body with.

God, this shirt represents all the messiness of our relationship.

Rory was right last night. We need to stop using each other as a crutch. We need to figure out how to be in each other's lives without the complications of sex and unresolved feelings.

Even if those complications are the only times I feel truly alive anymore.

But right now, it's so hard to hold myself back.

She searches my face.

"I want you to be happy," she finally says.

And then she steps back.

Fuck.

I catch her wrist and pull her back against me. Fucking hell. "I don't want you to think that I'm not happy right now, helping you out."

She shrugs. "But you weren't happy when we were together, and I'm not going to forget that."

"Because—"

She keeps going, cutting me off. "On the other side of this, I owe you one, big time. Whatever you need."

"Roar, listen to me."

She presses her lips together, her gaze tightening up. Wary.

"I shouldn't have said that."

"Was it not true?"

I wince.

Her gaze turns suspiciously bright.

I can't make her cry on Christmas Fucking Eve. "It *was* true, months ago. I shouldn't have said it because I don't think I'd feel the same way now, if we had a redo."

"We don't," she says tightly. "We *won't*."

The message is clear as a bell. I won't have a second chance to break her heart. And we need to learn how to roll through these waves of past hurt feelings. "I understand."

"Do you?"

"I do." I swallow hard. "We're trying to be friends. We both want that. And it's complicated because we're navigating that while pretending to date. And that's on top of actually being exes who still..."

I trail off, because that last part shouldn't matter. It should be behind us.

"Who still what?" Rory's voice is so small and quiet.

I should ignore the question. Leave it be. Because there are a lot of ways to end that thought, and they're all dangerous.

We're exes who still care about each other. Want each other. Even maybe love each other, although it's not enough.

I curve over her. "Who still have really good chemistry."

She nods slowly. "Yeah. That."

We're close enough that I can see the flecks of gold in her brown eyes. Close enough that it would be nothing to lean in and—

"There you are," Dante booms.

We jump apart, Rory spinning around and pressing her hands to her cheeks. Me staring up at the sky for a sobering second before nodding at her dad. "Yep. You need help with something?"

"Just came to count trees."

"Eight," Rory says quickly.

"Seven," I correct. "Emma said her mom wanted one and they didn't have one strapped to their car when they left. I'll buy one for them and drop it off."

"Oh, I can do that, son." Dante claps me on the shoulder.

Rory mutters something about finding her sisters and practically sprints away.

I watch her go. Every moment of playing this role is both the best and worst kind of torture. I want her back in my arms, but I also don't want to lie to her family.

She comes to a stop when she reaches her sisters.

Dante follows my gaze, and his expression softens. "It's good to see them all together. Been a rough couple of days for Cassie."

"Yeah."

"Are you heading to the market with them?"

I scrub my hand over my jaw, thinking about the Bechdel Test—and the way I keep finding Rory in my arms. A bit of space this afternoon wouldn't be bad. "No, I'm going to let them have sister time. I have presents to deliver to my cousins, anyway. So I can drop off the tree. You don't need to do a final delivery."

"I don't mind." Then he clears his throat. "You know, Carmen and I always thought you and Rory would be married by now."

I rub the back of my neck. "It's not, um..."

"If money is an issue—"

My throat tightens. This is exactly the kind of conversation I need to avoid. "Dante—"

"I'm not pushing," he says quickly. "Just...we wouldn't want that to be what stands between you kids and a...what does Jules call it? A happy ever after."

What's standing between Rory and a happy ever after is her job, but I can't tell that to her dad.

"It's definitely complicated," I manage. "But we're okay for money."

"All right. Well, grab a tree for Emma and put it in the back of the truck. If you're going out, you might as well drop it off. I'll get their address for you."

I find the biggest remaining tree and heft it over my shoulder.

Rory catches my gaze as I stride to the delivery truck.

The dirty memories she whispered to me last night slam to the front of my mind.

It's good that she has plans with her sisters.

If she didn't, I'd find a way to drag her out for this delivery with me, and find an abandoned lane to park in. See if she can still ride my thigh the way she used to, back when she wasn't sure yet about going all the way, but we both wanted to get off together.

I sling the tree into the back of the truck, then go back to the sales hut to grab my vest and the keys.

Jules and Cassie are already debating what treats to buy at the market.

"Hey," Rory says sliding up against me. "Thanks. You know, for being here. For helping. For..." She gestures to the truck. "That's nice, what you thought of for Emma with the tree."

"She was real worried about ruining her mom's Christmas plans, you know?" I shrug. "Did you get their number? Maybe I can send them a photo of the tree on their porch."

"Yeah. I'll text it to you."

"Thanks."

She goes to say something else, then stops. Bites her lip and then shakes her head.

I lean in and brush my lips against her forehead. "Don't worry, Roar. I'm right where I want to be."

And despite all the pretending, the complications, and everything that remains painfully unresolved between us, I mean it with all of my heart.

Chapter 14

Rory

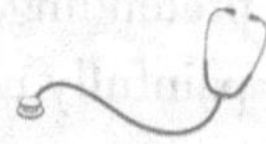

The Christmas market on Main Street is jam-packed when we pile off the wagon. Competing strains of Christmas music come from opposite ends of the street, and the unmistakeable scent of cinnamon sugar wafts out of Jules' favourite store on Main Street, the bakery enthusiastically named *Bake Sale!*

And because in Pine Harbour everyone is related to someone, the baker is Garrett's cousin-in-law.

"All right, let's divvy up our shopping list," I say, pulling out my phone to check the list Garett sent me. "Fancy crackers, cheese, crusty bread, apple cider donuts."

"That would be at the cider shack which is usually at the far end."

"Okay, let's head down there," I say, scanning the rest of what Mom needs.

As we start moving, a new message appears.

GARRETT

Tree delivered. How's the market?

Over the top festive, you'd hate it.

Jules grabs my phone. "No texting boyfriends during sister time! Bechdel Test!"

"Fine." I snatch it back. "But the list is in the text messages, so the best you get is a promise to ignore anything new he sends me."

We dive into the crowd, immediately getting separated by a gaggle of pink-cheeked kids in snowpants and toques chasing someone in an elf costume with candy canes in his pockets.

Jules snatches one of the candy canes and hands it to Cassie. "For you, Middle."

"Aw, thank you." She breaks it into three pieces and hands us each a part of the peppermint candy. "Hey, there's Rafe!"

Dani's oldest brother is just ahead of us with his wife and two kids.

He hears Cassie say his name and turns, a warm smile spreading across his face. "Hey there, cousins!"

We exchange hugs all around. Then the kids ask where Cassie got her candy cane.

She points to the elf, who's now dancing in front of the speakers.

"Okay, we better go catch him," Rafe says, winking. "See you on Boxing Day?"

"Absolutely," Jules says. "Bye, guys!" Then she nods down the street. "Onward to cider."

It takes us almost half an hour to navigate the crowd to the midpoint of the market, where the bakery is, because we keep getting happily distracted by stalls with yummy food and adorable Christmas decorations.

Only one person stops Cassie to ask about Nate, and Jules runs an interference play so aggressive, the poor woman blanches and scuttles away.

I consult the list again. "Bakery next?"

"There's probably a line," Jules says. "Do you want to keep going for cider donuts and we'll check it out?"

"Sounds good."

They disappear, and I shuffle forward. The couple in front of me is arguing about whether Die Hard counts as a Christmas movie, which makes me think of Garrett.

As if he can feel his ears burning, he sends me another message.

GARRETT

Just did the drive-by cousin elf thing.

RORY

If I go radio silent, it's because I'm being shamed for texting you.

GARRETT

Jules?

RORY

Who else?

GARRETT

Are you hiding from her right now?

RORY

Something like that.

GARRETT

How festive.

"Is that Garrett?" Cassie asks, appearing at my elbow.

I jump and look for Jules.

Cassie shakes her head as she laughs. "I left her in line, because it's wrapped around the corner. Let's go get the stuff Mom wants and then we'll meet up with her again. And it's okay if you're texting Garrett the whole time. I'm not offended."

Still, I put my phone away. "I definitely don't need to be. But it's good to hear you laughing, Middle."

We wander through the market, accumulating red pepper jelly and bacon jam, and two kinds of artisanal crackers from a pop-up shop called the *Laughing Ladle*.

"Do you think it's weird they don't sell soup?" Cassie asks after we move on.

"Mmm. And it's also strange that their ladle logo isn't laughing."

Jules joins us, swinging a bakery bag, as we lean on each other, cackling hysterically. "What did I miss?"

"Soup," Cassie wheezes.

"And I texted Garrett a bunch," I admit.

"No cookies for you." Jules wiggles her fingers. "Hand over your phone."

"I'm going to the cheese stall," Cassie says before disappearing.

"I'm handing this over willingly," I say.

The phone vibrates the second it hits Jules' palm. She eyes me. "The two of you are pathologically entwined."

We don't even live together, I want to admit. *You wouldn't have to scroll back very far to see that.* Instead, I deflect. "It could be Mom."

She checks. "It's him. He says he's back at the farm now."

"No other update?"

She shows me the screen.

A queer little feeling I don't want to name flutters in my belly.

"Do you want to dictate a reply?"

"No." Yes is the real answer. I want to drop a thumbs up on the update, and fire back a micro update of my own. Something small enough to not be necessary to send, but just sharing because once upon a time, we shared everything. We loved everything. We *were* entwined, and it wasn't pathological at all.

I hate that we lost that.

I hate that so, so much.

But today, this afternoon, is *not* the time for that.

Bechdel Fucking Test.

Jules puts the phone in her pocket, oblivious to my inner turmoil.

We find Cassie deep in conversation with a young woman at the cheese stand.

We wander to the thrifted goods stall next door, and a red sparkly vest catches Jules' eye. We stop so she can inspect it and that's when I see a kitchen timer in the shape of a garishly painted chicken.

And it winds up to exactly ninety minutes.

"What's that?" Jules asks, looking over my shoulder.

I test it out to see if it works. It starts...making clucking sounds.

"Oh my God," she says when I hold it up for the vendor to give me a price. "Why?"

We've talked about Garrett enough.

And I don't want to have to explain why an objectively weird gift is the perfect present for him this season.

Knowing Jules, she'll just ask if I'm mad at him, and wouldn't that be ironic.

I was, for so long. But even the little flare of resentment I had when we were counting trees faded away pretty quickly.

"Bechdel Test," I simply say as I hand over money for both the timer and the cocktails book.

And then Cassie joins us.

"You got cheese?" I ask.

"So much cheese."

"Cider next?"

Jules links arms with me on one side, and Cassie on the other. "I mean, *yes*, finally!"

Chapter 15

Garrett

I'm stretching out on Rory's bed, reading, when the girls get back from the market.

She comes barrelling in, then pulls up short when she sees me, and shoves her hands behind her back. "Oh! Hi. You're here."

I swing my legs off the bed. "I was taking a break."

"Can you close your eyes?"

"Sure." I blink my eyelids shut and listen to her rustle around. A drawer opens, then closes. "What are you doing?"

"Hiding something small I got you at the market." She comes closer, until she's standing right in front of me.

I keep my eyes shut.

She steps in between my legs, her knee brushing against the inside of mine. Nudging my thighs wider.

Reflexively, my hands come up to her hips.

"Is this okay?" My voice is low and rough. Can she hear the need there? Fuck. "Maybe blurs the lines of friendship. You said you didn't want—"

"I know what I said. But this might be the last chance

we get to be alone, so...." Her fingertips ghost over my lips. Her hands push against my shoulders as she leans in, her soft sweater so close it's tickling my jaw. Her lips brush my ear. "If you keep your eyes shut, and just let me play with you, it's sort of like it's not really happening."

"I promise you that it feels very, very real."

"Do you want me to stop?"

Fuck no. "I didn't say that."

She exhales, sweet apple cider and secret need swirling around me. "I don't want you to think I only ask you to scratch an itch when it's overwhelming." Her hands trail down my chest. "I don't want you to think I'm...selfish."

With a gentle shove, she sends me tumbling back.

I blink my eyes open and stare up at the ceiling as she unbuckles my belt.

"Your family," I manage to get out, rolling my head up to look at her.

She wraps her hand around my bare cock and shrugs.

Shrugs.

"I guess you'll have to be quiet?"

I choke on a laugh as she licks around the straining crown, my surging erection. All for her. Only for her.

Her thumb rubs up and down over my piercings, and the pleased hum she makes as she chases that touch with her whole mouth is so damn good. She swallows me so those bars run right over her tongue, and fuck that feels good. Great. Incredible.

Mind-fucking-blowing.

She's definitely not selfish. Rory Minelli is a very, very giving human being. "My *God.*"

"Goddess, if you please," she says, her breath warm against the slick wetness coating my shaft. "Or Roar, if you want. I like hearing you moan my name."

"I can't moan your name. People will know what you're doing." My chest heaves as I shove my fingers into her hair and guide her back down my cock. "Don't stop sucking, for the love of—"

She closes her lips around me and *pulls*. My eyes roll back in my head, and I have to bite my lip to keep the sounds I'm making inside my body.

"Your mouth is so perfect," I manage to whisper. There, that's the right now. Low and private, just for her ears. "You're so good at that, Roar. You make me feel so fucking good. Are you going to swallow my seed? Want me to spill like this? Or do you want to stroke me and see me come all over your hand and my piercings?"

She pops off, her eyes wild and bright. She holds my gaze as she pumps my cock. "Yeah, make a mess for me."

Fuck fuck fuck.

Climb on top of me, I want to beg. *Let me make a mess inside you.*

Instead, I stare at her, transfixed, as she strokes her thumb up and down the underside of my shaft, my cock throbbing in her tight hold. I'm sure my eyes are just as hot and wild as hers, just as dangerously close to spilling secrets that would ruin this new peace we've navigated towards.

But I can't look away.

My hips buck into her touch, my balls pulling tight. Churning with desire, with need, with something so profoundly *right* that I hate how much I fucked us up.

This could have been something so good, and I lost sight of that. I forgot how to be hers, and I wasted an entire year of our lives.

It's really fucking something that I'm still fucking her hand while feeling that regret so intensely. As if sex is all that matters. It's not even close, but I will take every second of intimacy I can get with her, on her terms, because it's so much better than nothing.

And the sight of her mouth stretched wide around me, the feel of my barbells and her tongue, the quiet, urgent sucking sounds, the soft slide of her curls through my fingers as she bobs her head and holds her eyes on my face...it's all perfect, actually.

"I'm not going to last."

She smiles around my cock, as if to say *good*. As if that's the point.

She wants to make me explode on her tongue.

So I give in and let her take me there. My balls draw tighter, tighter, then clench up, pulsing pure pleasure as she gulps down my release.

So. Fucking. Good.

"You're incredible, just the best, holy shit," I whisper.

She pulls off and grins. "Great job being quiet."

I laugh and tug at her arm. "Get up here."

"No, that was just for you." She licks her lips, her eyes glowing. "Because I appreciate you."

Ah, of course. She has a righteous sense of fairness, and she wouldn't want to owe me too much for being kind over the holidays. But if we're going to have transactional sex, it's going to be fair in its own way.

"Returning the pleasure would also be for me," I growl as I catch her by the arm, then find the strength to lever myself up and grab her hips so I can tumble her onto the bed. "Now it's your turn to be quiet."

"I need to change the sheets and get—"

"Shut up and let me lick your pussy, Roar."

She shuts up.

I tug her waistband down, kissing the softness of her

belly, nosing my way to the start of her pubic hair, those secret dark curls that are just for me.

She lifts her hips, because even though she thought she wanted to just be giving, she secretly craves this, too.

We both do.

I peel her leggings to her knees, then yank her panties down. My hunger mounts as I glimpse a betraying glisten along her slit.

"Did sucking my pierced cock get you wet, Roar?" I flip her over and pull her up onto her knees. "Why would you want to go downstairs with an aching little cunt when I could make you feel good?"

"I thought—"

"Stop thinking," I demand. "Push your face into the sheets and just *feel*."

She starts to protest, but as soon as I take her ass in my hands, tipping her hips up so I can get to her sweet little pussy, she gives in.

All the fight softens out of her and she whimpers into the sheets, the sweetest sound ever.

"That's it," I whisper. "You want my tongue, you feisty girl?"

"Mm-hmm."

"Can you be quiet?"

"No."

I laugh at the honesty, my breath brushing against her slick skin. "That's your choice, then. I don't care if they hear how good I make you feel."

She squirms, her hips wriggling in my hands. I squeeze and lift her flesh, revealing more of her sweetness.

"Please, Garrett," she pants.

"Love to hear you beg," I rumble before finally giving her what she needs.

She's sweet and tart on my tongue, and so fucking responsive. A day and a half of us not touching each other has primed her just as much as ovulating would. My needy, greedy, horny girl.

Her clit leaps to attention when I lick around it, throbbing as I latch on to suck.

Why the fuck haven't we been doing this all the fucking time?

I growl and dive deeper, tonguing her entrance, her folds, and her clit again. I lap and lick and suck until she's trembling, and then I latch my whole mouth onto her and *consume* her like she's my last fucking meal.

"We need to strip the sheets."

"What's that, Miss Mumbles?"

Rory twists her head and looks at me where I've stretched out beside her. Her cheeks are so flushed—it's fucking beautiful. "You heard me."

"We will. But we can take a minute to enjoy the aftershocks."

She takes a breath and holds it.

I shake my head. "Don't say we shouldn't have done that. We clearly both wanted it."

"It's just—"

"It's Christmas Eve. Whatever that was, it was festive." I'll use her love of the holidays against her, I don't care. "If you want to do it again tonight in front of the Christmas tree, I won't mind."

"You won't *mind*?"

"I'm playing it cool. Wouldn't want you to know how desperate I am do it again."

She smiles despite herself.

"Yeah, you like that, don't you?" I grin back.

She rolls onto her back and tugs her leggings up and over her hips again. "They'll be here soon."

The second attempt to redirect us back to the task of making sure the Minelli Family Christmas is perfect.

Note taken.

"All right." I roll off the bed. "What do we need to do in here?"

"They'll bring a playpen for the boys to sleep in, so we just need to get our bags out of here." Her eyes soften. "I, um, bought you a present I need to wrap, too."

I clutch at my chest. "A present and you came on my face? I am not worthy."

"Shut up." But she's giggling. "Can you go grab a set of sheets from the hallway closet? And knock when you come back but I'll wrap it quickly."

I take a detour through the bathroom to wash my face and hands. I'd keep Rory imprinted on my skin all afternoon if we weren't going to be hugging family members any minute.

Then I find fresh linens.

When I return, she's added a newly wrapped present to the top of the bag of gifts.

She tracks my gaze. "It's just something small. It's okay if you didn't—"

"I got you something, too."

"Oh." She jerks her eyes to the sheets in my hand. "Let's make the bed."

"I got it. Why don't you pack up your clothes for our move downstairs? Everything of mine is still in my bag."

She turns to the dresser, but as soon as I pull the blanket and the sheets off the bed, she's back, trying to insert herself into the task.

Irritation flares. "I'm perfectly capable of making a bed, Rory."

She doesn't even look at me. "I know you are."

"Do you?" I mutter under my breath.

"What does that mean?"

"Nothing."

She snatches a pillow and yanks off the pillowcase. "Didn't sound like nothing."

I know that Rory knows I can make a bed. "I don't know where that came from."

"It's just what we do. We made it a lot longer than ninety minutes, though, so..." She closes her eyes and takes a long, deep breath. "It's okay."

"Yeah. We're both probably on edge." Except I thought the orgasms would help with that. But on the other side of them there's just more tension.

"And I just want it to be—" She stops and presses her lips together.

"What? Perfect?"

"Good." But she glances away.

I cross my arms over my chest, trying to ignore the tension coiling in my shoulders. "It's not your job to make Christmas perfect for your family."

Her cheeks heat up, annoyed. "It's not *not* my job. I mean, ideally it's everyone's job. I know you don't care—"

"You don't think I care about making sure you have a good Christmas? And your family by extension?"

"No, I mean—"

"Because I'm *here*."

"I *know that*. I see that! I'm saying, it's not something

you care about. The holidays. I know you're doing it for me. But that makes it all the more stressful in a way, which is why I want to even the balance out!"

We glare at each other. Her eyes are locked on mine, and I can see the struggle in them—the push and pull between what she really wants and what she thinks she *should* want. Or maybe what she thinks she needs.

God knows, I have no clue what she needs. Not really. Not anymore. And I know she doesn't want to be mine, but I still don't know *why*.

"Garrett," she says, her voice barely above a whisper.

I shift closer. Too close, my body humming with the need to touch her again. "I don't want to stress you out, Roar. I always want to ease your burdens, because you're precious to me, and if this isn't the way—"

A door slams on the first level, and the unmistakable high-pitched laughter of small children drifts up the stairs.

She pushes me away. "They're here."

"Hang on a second," I say, heart pounding.

But she's gone, slipping past me the way she always slides out of my grasp. The way she slid out of my life when I told her I wasn't happy anymore.

Rory Minelli has an intense self-preservation instinct.

And deep down, I scare her.

Chapter 16

Rory

You're precious to me.
What the fuck is that?
What the actual fuck is that?

Chapter 17

Garrett

By the time I get downstairs with my backpack over my shoulder, Carmen's sisters are both in the kitchen, and there's a double dose of laughing sister trios, all talking over each other. It's a cacophony of noise. I make eye contact with Tabitha's husband and wave before he ducks back outside, presumably to bring in their bags and all the toddler gear.

Rory, on the other hand, is notably dodging eye contact. I watch intently as she picks up one of the little boys racing around the kitchen, and he giggles as she whispers something to him.

She doesn't look over, even though I'm sure she can feel my gaze burning into her skin.

"You look freshly rumpled," Jules says as she appears beside me, Mara right behind her.

I manage not to jump out of my skin *and* ignore the pointed observation. "Merry Christmas, Aunt Mara."

"You, too. I hope you haven't been behaving yourself."

"He's been getting up to all sorts of trouble," Jules promises, speaking for me with an exaggerated lie. The only trouble I've been getting up to this year is constantly re-inserting myself into Rory's bullshit like a glutton for punishment.

I pointedly change the subject and ask Mara about her daughter. "No Glory this year?"

"She's *working*, can you imagine?"

Of course Mara is horrified at the thought, but Glory is her opposite in many ways.

"Christmas break is a good time to pick up extra shifts," I point out, and then think, *I could have done the same.*

"That's what she said." Mara shakes her head. "Well, it's her time."

I smile. "How is she liking university?"

"Loves it. Just loves it."

"That's great." I glance back at Rory. She still has one of the twins on her hip.

Mara follows my gaze, then smiles.

Damn it.

"I need to..." I pull out my phone, and there's a text message on the screen that helps me extract myself from this conversation. "We had a skater break her arm earlier today. I was going to say I need to check on her, but her mom has sent an update, so excuse me for a minute."

"Of course."

I carry my bag into the back room and stash it beside one of the couches, then I click into the message. It's a photo of Emma and her parents in front of the tree I left on their porch. Emma's arm is in a cast, but she's smiling now.

I send back a quick *Merry Christmas* to them, then take a deep breath as I hear another raucous peel of laughter ring out.

Chapter 18

Rory

Garrett doesn't come back immediately. I hate how much I want to follow him into the back room. I'm going to resist *that* instinct, though.

I can't run away from him and then chase after him. I need to slow down and just be more...careful.

"What should we do first?" Jules asks. "Make boozy eggnog? Decorate cookies?"

"Eggnog," Mara says.

"Cookies," the twins scream. One of them right in my ear.

Wincing, I set him down. "Definitely eggnog."

The kids climb onto the kitchen chairs, making them my mom's problem as Cassie catches our aunts up on her separation, without giving any details. Jules and I escape to the liquor cabinet.

"Do you think they fought about kids?" Jules asks under her breath.

"They who?"

"Cassie and Nate."

I do a double take. "What? Why do you think that?"

"Dunno. Just a vibe." She pulls out a bottle of brandy. "This?"

"And maybe rum, too."

"How about you guys? Do you and Garrett ever fight about kids?"

I think about what he said in the truck on the drive here. "We used to. Not that I realized it at the time."

"What does that mean?" Jules finds a bottle of spiced rum.

I grab the shaker.

Arms full, we cross to the counter closest to the fridge.

"We need cinnamon and nutmeg," I tell her.

She finds the spices, then grabs the shaker from me and immediately adds ice.

"Not yet," I tell her.

She ignores me and starts free pouring booze.

I roll my eyes and cover the eggs as she reaches for them. "Baby, you don't shake the eggs with ice."

"How was I supposed to know?"

"Literally by reading the recipe?"

"I skimmed it."

"Get the hand mixer. We might as well make a big batch, anyway, because I bet Dad will drink a few."

I start separating egg yolks from the whites, and by the time she's found the mixer, I have the yolks in a bowl with cream, milk, and sugar, and the whites in a separate bowl.

Holding out my hand, I use my bossiest big sister energy to demand the appliance. She lets me take that part over, but my punishment is more questions about having babies.

"Garrett wants kids and you don't," she says under the loud whir of the motor, as if that's a statement of fact. It's not.

"I wanted to wait more than he did. And so the default is waiting."

"He was watching you when you had one of the twins on your hip."

I ignore the flash of heat that zaps through me, burning like I've just done a shot of the spiced rum. "He was probably wondering how such a small person could make so much noise."

"You or the child?"

I test the egg whites. "Shut up."

"So are you still waiting?"

I know it's an innocent question—as innocent as nosy Jules can ever be. She thinks Garrett and I are still together, and I just said that we both wanted kids...at some point.

"It's complicated," I manage to say around a lump in my throat. "This is pretty good. Let's switch bowls."

She lets me focus on making the nog. Once the yolk mixture is creamy, I fold everything together. "Now let's add the booze."

Jules goes to dump in the shaker, ice and all.

"No! Strain it off—" Suddenly frustrated, I grab the shaker and do it myself.

Jules stares at me, brow furrowed.

"We need four more shots of each," I snap.

"Ooo-kay."

She measures them out, and she's just dumped in the last one when Garrett returns.

Ignoring the way my heart leaps, I give him what I hope is an easy smile and casual eye contact that doesn't betray how hard it is to play it cool.

But I need to put on a chill front, or my sister is going to ask even more awkward questions.

"Eggnog's almost ready," I tell him out loud. And I also try to silently, subtly convey that my sister is being nosy.

He smoothes his hand up and down my spine. "Looks good."

"Rory was very bossy about how to make it," Jules mutters.

"I've missed this," I say brightly. "Me being right, all this festive magic, etcetera etcetera."

"Definitely missed all this," Garrett says, looking at me as he says it, and my heart twists. But then he smirks. "Etcetera. What can I do to help?"

All my instinctive answers to that question are indecent. And inappropriate. "Do you know where my dad is?"

"Last I saw, he was helping Allan bring in bags from the car. I'll go find them and let them know that eggnog is ready." He pats my shoulder as he leaves again. "And you should drink some water."

Jules watches him go, then narrows her eyes at me. "What's going on with you guys?"

I wince as Mara immediately shifts her gaze to us.

Without the cover of the hand mixer, it feels like Jules yelled that to the entire room, and now Mom and her sisters and Cassie are all staring at me.

"Eggnog's ready," I say brightly.

Mom frowns. "Oh no, Rory, you aren't—" She glances at the twins and mouths something I don't understand, "—too, are you?"

"What?"

"Mom, no." Jules grimaces, apparently more fluent in Mom lipreading. "That's not how you use that."

"Use what?" Tabitha looks back and forth between them.

"Dickmatized," my Mom says dramatically.

Silence falls over the kitchen.

Then we all burst out laughing, and it builds as the word bounces around in my head, rent-free. *Dickmatized.*

"No?" She looks so confused.

That only makes us laugh harder.

"My sides hurt," I gasp.

Cassie wipes her eyes. "Mom, what do you think that means?"

"You're traumatized by dick." Mom's forehead crinkles.

"Oh," Cassie says, and that single syllable sends us all howling again.

"No?"

She shakes her head. "No. It's *hypnotized* by dick. Like it's that good. So literally the opposite."

"Oh." Mom laughs at herself. "Well, I shouldn't have said that, then."

Jules cackles. "No."

"It's good that you weren't so dickmatized by Nate that you couldn't leave him."

"Mom!" Cassie waves her hands.

"What? Still no?"

"Very much no," Jules says. "Nobody wants to think about Nate's penis."

"I do," Mara says. She shrugs when we all stare at her. "What? If he wasn't good enough to Cassie, then we should talk about that. You girls need to stand up for your own pleasure."

Cassie buries her face in her hands. "Make it stop."

Tabitha gestures at my mom. "Cookie decorating, Carmie?"

"Yes, of course. Rory, hurry up with the drinks."

"I was trying to when you took this in a weird direction!"

Just then, the guys all come back, and that sends everyone into another wave of hysterical laughter that nobody is willing to explain.

Garrett's gaze immediately finds me, and the wild giggle dies on my tongue. His eyebrows lift in a silent question. *Having fun?*

Yes. The answer is immediate and unreservedly true. I smile and nod.

The corners of his mouth curve up, and all the breath rushes out of me. I stare at him, the noise of the kitchen fading away.

I don't know why a simple smile has tilted my world on its axis, but here we are.

It's like I'm seeing Garrett through fresh eyes.

Jules nudges me, and I drag my attention to the glasses she's set out. I manage to pour a round of drinks, and then we all raise our glasses to sister in-jokes.

My heart is pounding as I take a sip of my nog. It's delicious. The wild warmth spreading through my limbs isn't from the rum, though. That's all Garrett.

Chapter 19

Garrett

I'm *very* aware of Rory being *very* aware of me, and it's killing me that I can't drag her away to talk about whatever is going on in her busy, pretty little head. I probably pushed too far by telling her that she's precious to me, but fuck it, it's true. And if there's a chance in hell that the truth gets us somewhere better, then that would be fucking amazing.

But Christmas Eve isn't the time for private conversations. It's not even time for uninterrupted group conversations. The sisters all talk over each other, both generations, and none of them seem bothered. They understand each other's half-sentences and find everything hilarious.

It's nice to see Rory laugh this much.

I've missed that.

After eggnog, Carmen tries to decorate cookies with the young monsters, but that makes a massive mess.

"I bet Uncle Dante could find you some lights to decorate a tree with outside, hmm?" she finally says. When your family owns a Christmas tree farm, there's never an end to the decorating possibilities. "Do you boys want to go outside with your dad and Garrett?"

I'm not sure why I'm being volunteered for this, other than the fact that I'm tall, and a guy, but I don't mind. Whatever the Minellis need today, I'm their dude.

Rory's sisters stay inside with their mom and Aunt Tabitha, but to my surprise, she comes outside with us—and her Aunt Mara comes out, too, wearing an oversized puffy winter coat that looks, at first, like it's paint-splattered.

"You're staring, Garrett," she teases me. "I didn't actually paint in it, you know."

"I *was* wondering."

"It's a limited edition version of this coat, featuring my work."

Rory gasps as her aunt twirls around. "Way to bury the lede, Aunt Mara!"

"Isn't it fun?" The older woman grins. "The royalties paid for Glory's tuition this year."

Dante interrupts us to ask me to get a ladder from the tree lot.

When I get back with it, Dante and Allan—and the boys—are nowhere to be seen.

"There was a meltdown," Rory says. "So they went in search of a spotlight to help Santa find the chimney."

"Ah." I lean the ladder against the first tree.

"And how are you two doing?" Mara asks. Her sharp artist's eyes take in more than I'd like. "You look relaxed."

Heat creeps up Rory's cheeks. "It's nice to be home."

"Mmm." Her gaze flicks back and forth between us. "I bet it is. And how are you finding being chief resident?"

"It's a lot of work."

"Carmen was saying that Garrett takes good care of you, though?"

Fuck my life.

Rory bites her lip.

"I try," I say.

She nods. "He's always there when I need him, yeah."

"What about you?" Mara asks me. "Are you still juggling the garage and the army?"

"Yep, I am."

"And he started playing rugby," Rory bursts out.

Her dad returns as she says that. "Did you, Garrett?"

That leads to a lengthy conversation about the different kinds of rugby, studded with toddler demands for more lights.

The whole time, Rory's cheeks are pink.

And when we all finally head back inside for fondue and charcuterie and an obscene amount of chocolate, I catch her hand and tug her back, so we're the last ones to go inside.

"What?" She asks, whirling around. Eyes bright.

"I know we gotta get in there, too." I draw her close. Just for a second. Heart pounding in my throat. "We didn't get to finish our conversation earlier. And I know now isn't the time, either. But tonight...after everyone has gone to bed...I think we should talk. I want to talk more, about us."

Her breath puffs out into the cold air, the temperature dipping down below freezing now that the sun is set. "Us?"

"Yeah, I—"

The door pushes open behind her. Jules pokes her head out. "Stop kissing and get in here!"

I don't let go of Rory. "We'll be right there."

"We're not kissing," Rory says over her shoulder, but her eyes stay locked on my face.

And maybe that's the problem.

The rest of Christmas Eve spirals from there. Chaotic, noisy, slightly exasperating. But underneath all of that is a low sizzle of anticipation for bedtime, when everyone else is finally quiet, finally asleep, and I can pin Rory down.

Maybe literally.

Roll her beneath me on the old couch and make her talk about her fears.

By the time people start to head upstairs, it's all I can think about. A couple of glasses of egg nog have dulled my responses, too, so I don't clue in fast enough when Rory's dad hangs back when she goes into the downstairs bathroom to change into her best Christmas pyjamas.

"You know, Garrett," Dante says. "I was thinking about what we talked about earlier."

I frown in confusion. "The tree decorating?"

"No." He chuckles good-naturedly. "The question of a wedding—"

"Yeah, no, we don't need to talk about that now," I say quickly, shaking my head.

"No, I know you kids will do it your own way, but I've been thinking about repurposing the barn into an event space. It would be nice to have a wedding here, I'm just saying. Maybe next summer."

Behind him, there's a crash, and Rory comes stumbling out of the bathroom in the most dramatic, she-definitely-heard-that reaction.

I hold up my hands. "It's nothing."

Dante laughs. "Getting married isn't *nothing*, son. I know you said that it's not about money, but if we can make it easier on you, then that's a good thing." He glances back and forth between me and Rory. "Right?"

I don't answer him.

Rory doesn't answer him.

She looks *furious*.

"Rory and I haven't talked about it," I finally say, because that's the truth.

He sighs and turns to go upstairs, but stops beside his daughter. "Oh, Aurora. Don't leave this one hanging for too long. You might lose him."

All the blood drains from her face.

Fuuuuck.

As soon as he's gone, I try to make it right, but she doesn't let me get very many words out. "That's not—"

"Let's just go to bed," she mutters, her gaze determinedly focused on the shorter of the two couches, now made up into a bed for her.

Fury rises. "What about talking?"

"I don't want to *talk*," she snaps.

This isn't healthy, the way that we fight, how angry I get when she pulls away, how she snarls when she's feeling defensive.

But I've spent the last few months thinking a lot about the why of it all, and I don't believe for a second that Rory is mad at me when she snaps. I think she's scared.

I just don't know what she's scared about.

"I don't think that's true. I think you're mad that we didn't talk earlier, that you were blindsided just now."

She shrugs her shoulders in a tight acknowledgement that I'm on the right track.

I take a deep breath. "Earlier today, your dad asked me if I needed money for an engagement ring. If that was why we aren't married yet."

She snorts. "And you decided not to tell me about that."

"Yeah."

That gets her full attention.

She jerks her head up and glares at me. "That's some nerve, keeping something like that from me."

"What would telling you have accomplished? It didn't bother me that he asked. I told him we're fine for money, and that was the end of that."

"It gave him the idea—" She cuts herself off.

I raise my brows. "What, that we're together?"

Her gaze sparks, a warm ember glowing suddenly very hot and very bright. I shouldn't enjoy that as much as I do. The way it heats her up from the inside out, making her cheeks pink and her chest heave.

But it's so close to how she looks when she's turned on.

She even said as much, that she likes getting mad because it takes her to this space, where she shuts off her brain and just feels. And I really like making Rory feel things.

"Look, I get that this was my terrible idea, but you don't need to dig us into an even deeper hole," she says hotly.

"Ah." I step closer, because this is a conversation that can't carry up the stars. This is private. "You don't want to give anyone the idea that I'm over the moon in love with you. Together, yes. Happy, no. That's the status quo we need to maintain."

"Exactly." Her eyes *blaze* now.

"Because at some point soon we're going to be very publicly over."

Chapter 20

Rory

Why does Garrett have to put it like that? But he's not wrong.

I swallow hard around the lump in my throat. "Yes."

The corners of his mouth turn down.

I hate the traitorous hope in my chest. "What are you thinking?"

"I'm not." His words are clipped, though.

"It's not something we need to do this weekend." I back up, my legs bumping into the shorter of the two couches down here. My couch.

All I can think is, I'm going to miss sleeping next to him.

I slept so well last night, damn it.

He turns and grabs his bag. "I'm going to get changed."

I avert my gaze as he unbuckles his belt and peels off his jeans. Not completely, of course. I can still see his long, strong legs out of the corner of my eye. *Hello, rugby thighs.*

They *are* more muscular than before.

Before.

He pulls on a pair of sweatpants.

Good night, rugby thighs.

Then he peels off his t-shirt.

Hello, sexy back.

I shouldn't covet him like this. It's not going to make breaking up again any easier, even if I take the coward's way out and just inform my family via text message, maybe mid-January, that unfortunately Garrett and I have decided to part ways.

What I should I have done last April.

This is what I get for procrastinating to avoid the mess. I get even more mess.

I finally manage to tear my eyes away as he slides on a clean t-shirt for bed—*goodnight, sexy back*—and I try to get comfortable in my makeshift bed.

Across the room, he stashes his bag away, then glances my way.

I stare at the ceiling.

"You think I should have told you earlier that he asked me about a wedding?" he finally asks.

My shoulders tighten up and I try not to hunch them towards my ears. "You don't?"

"Nope." Unapologetic, resolutely calm. So Garrett of him.

I twist the edge of my blanket in my fingers. "Why not?"

There's a rustle as he gets settled on his couch. Then he says, "Because it wasn't emotional for me, but it would have been for you."

I press my lips together. He'd already said as much, but to hear him say it again, and more explicitly...he's right, and that's a surprise. I'm emotional now just thinking about it. And he's not, even about something that he claims he wanted very much.

Maybe he didn't.

Maybe that's why I pushed him away, even though he's the only one I want close.

"Stop thinking that I don't care," he mutters.

I gasp. "Excuse me?"

"I can hear you."

"No you can't."

"You're stewing so hard the whole room is vibrating."

"Well maybe I'm thinking there's a reason why you aren't emotional about it!"

"Yeah?"

"Yes."

"Come over here and tell me all about it."

I huff. "You'd like that."

"Yeah, I would."

I jerk my head sideways and glare at him. He's on his side, his head propped up on his hand. And his expression is entirely unreadable. It sends my insides into free fall.

"Get over here," he says, patting the cushion in front of him.

I swallow hard. "We won't both fit."

"We'll fit just fine."

"I'm mad at you."

"You're always mad at me. But I don't think you want your family involved in this fight, so maybe you should come over here and be mad at me in a more up-close, quiet kind of way."

I push the blanket off me and sit up. "We're not fooling around."

He shrugs. "Sure."

"Garrett—"

He holds out his hand.

Heart in my throat, I cross to him and let him tug me

down to the couch, where I very annoyingly fit right into the crook of his arm.

He covers me with his blanket. "I've heard that it's more comfortable to be mad when you're cozy."

"Shut up," I mutter.

But I still burrow deeper against his body, soaking up his strength and his heat. It's a bittersweet kind of comfort, because I know it's stolen, that last night was supposed to be our final night together in a bed.

Just like I was supposed to be relieved that tonight we each had a separate couch, but I lasted less than five minutes before scurrying into his arms.

Maybe I won't spend the *entire* night like this.

He's right that we shouldn't bicker across the living room. If we need to have a conversation, we can do it close up.

And then I'll go back to my own couch.

"I'm not always mad at you," I whisper. It seems like a good place to start.

"I wouldn't blame you if you were. I broke us up."

"Because we weren't happy."

"Yeah."

"Seems like a good reason to break up."

"I thought so." But then he takes a deep breath, his whole chest lifting, pressing against my back. And I hear the doubt, loud and clear.

I try to twist around, to look at him, but he bands his arm around my waist, holding me where I am.

"Can I tell you something?" His breath is warm against my temple.

"Of course."

"I regret breaking us up. I'm not saying it was wrong, because I don't think it was, but... Once you know how quiet, how completely *silent* loneliness is, it really puts what you once had in a new perspective."

"Oh." I close my eyes to keep the hot press of tears at bay. "I have regrets, too, you know."

"You want to share?"

"I regret letting you think I didn't want to get married."

"Did you, though?"

"Yes."

"What about waiting?"

"That's the thing. I wanted that, too. And now I know that I can't have it both ways." I suck in a quick breath. "This is so hard."

"It's probably harder because it's also your favourite time of year."

It's probably too self-pitying to tell him that it's been agonizingly hard every single day since he left.

Yeah, that's too much.

So I just nod.

He rubs his face into my hair. "New Year's resolution to let go of regret?"

"Yeah. No more what-ifs about an apple orchard wedding."

"That's fucking specific."

I shrug. "Doesn't matter now. Plus being specific helps let it go, maybe?"

"Sure. I can buy that." He makes a humming, thinking sound. "Okay, I regret not kissing you during our hookups."

"What?" This time, he lets me twist around. I nearly fall off the couch, but he catches me and pulls me back against him once I've turned over. "Where is that coming from?"

"Every time you summoned me—"

"I didn't summon you!"

His eyes crinkle at my protest. "Potato potahtoh."

"You *offered*."

"Still. Either way, I felt like I shouldn't kiss you. That wasn't what we did anymore." His jaw moves, then his throat bobs up and down. I'm close enough to catalogue every little part of his visceral reactions to his own confession. "But when this is over, if I'm going to do a postmortem on it, that'll be my biggest regret. Not kissing you more when I knew that every time might be our last time. I didn't make it the most it could be, and I regret holding back."

How am I supposed to respond to that?

"I thought the same thing, you know," I whisper. "That every time might be our last. It actually haunted me that I couldn't remember our last time before...you know."

"The summoning?"

"The offering."

"Mmm." His brow furrows. "I think it was in the middle of the night."

"Yeah, probably." I swallow and focus my eyes on his mouth.

We stare at each other, a warm tangle of limbs and regret. In the narrow space between us, my heart hammers in a wild, irregular rhythm. His confession has done something funny to the self-preservation I've held onto for too long. It's as if he's shared a new piece of his heart, raw and unadulterated. Regret feels like too shallow a word for what is tightening in my chest, sharp at the edges and brittle all the way through.

I might shatter.

But his emerald-flecked gaze is steady.

I breathe through the pound of my pulse as his gaze anchors me. And I tighten my fingers into the front of his soft t-shirt.

He exhales, his breath meeting mine in a gust of permission I didn't know I needed until we both lean in at the same time.

I'm sure I kiss him first, but it's mutual, a soft collision of lips. Uncertain and wary, because after all this time, we're strangers who don't do this. But then need grows and familiarity follows, hesitancy melting into an urgent fever.

We taught each other how to kiss, once upon a time.

And then, for a long time, it was just something nice that we did—and we did it often. Daily, until we stopped. Until anger and unhappiness made us stop.

Somewhere in there, I forgot that Garrett Kincaid is a master at this thing he once learned with me.

Oh *Lord*, can this man kiss. His lips part mine and his tongue strokes deep. His hand cradles my face, holding me as he swallows my whimpers for the first time in eight months. Little desperate sounds that I can't hold in because his cock is straining against my belly, and only a few layers of soft cotton separate us. I wriggle closer.

"We're not fooling around," he grinds out between tastes. "It's Christmas Eve, you hot little thing."

I laugh and kiss him back.

No, no fooling around tonight.

But no more fighting, either. Just kisses, endless kisses, making up for lost time. And then a sweet, hot, snuggly drift into a very hopeful sleep.

Chapter 21

Garrett

For the second day in a row, I wake up with a hard cock and a handful of warm, sleepy tit.

Ah fuck, I think, immediately followed by, *she feels so good, though*.

Unlike yesterday, I don't have the luxury of holding Rory for a moment, of enjoying how soft and sweet she is, because what woke me up was the thunder of tiny footsteps above us.

Her toddler cousins are awake.

"Roar," I murmur.

She whines in protest and wiggles her bum against my cock.

Fucking hell, I agree, we should stay exactly where we are. "We can't be caught like this."

Even though I'd put up with all the teasing in the world, and everyone thinks we're still together anyway. But she's never been one for PDAs.

Last night's kisses play in my head like an All Star highlight reel as I slide out from behind her.

We probably shouldn't have done that. I was right that

kissing was different than hooking up, and it complicates everything. But as soon as I confessed to her that I'd held back, as soon as she looked at my mouth with that hungry, unfiltered expression of pure need, I knew we were going to crash through that boundary. We needed to.

I'd do it again this morning if we weren't going to have company in three, two, one—

"Santa came!" The twins are like a tornado, spiralling into the room with completely chaotic intention.

I've just snatched the blanket and pillow from the couch that Rory didn't sleep on, and I'm holding them in front of my crotch as I give a gruff *good morning* nod to Allan and Tabitha, who are corralling their children to only open the presents that are for them.

Carmen follows quickly, bustling around the kitchen. I leave Rory sleeping and go to make myself useful.

I've just poured a cup of coffee when Rory stumbles into the kitchen, hair fluffy and eyes barely open.

I hold the mug in the air and she beelines for it, her hands outstretched.

"Good morning," I murmur as she collides into me.

She mumbles something as she pulls the coffee to her mouth.

I kiss the top of her head and wrap my arm around her waist, holding her close.

"How'd you sleep?" Carmen asks.

Rory's cheeks turn pink. "Great."

Then she slashes a quick glance up at me, checking to see if my answer is the same.

As if I would want to be anywhere but wrapped around her.

"Yeah, great. The couches are very comfortable." I clear my throat. "Need any help with breakfast?"

Every year it's the same thing, hashbrown casserole and cinnamon rolls, both of which Carmen has prepped in the fridge so they just need to be slid into the oven.

But I offer anyway, and she waves me off as she always does.

Over the next half hour, everyone else wakes up and joins us. After her first cup of coffee, Rory disappears to get showered and changed. She comes back wearing jeans and a silky pink top that shows off her tits and makes me want to howl at how many people are in this house right now.

When the cinnamon rolls come out of the oven, she's right there, waiting for the first one.

"You want to share?" she asks me over the din of her family serving themselves, holding up the plate.

More than anything. I pat the counter next to me, and when she comes over, I lift her up so she can sit next to me, so I can breathe in her sweet vanilla body wash and pretend that all of this is as real as it feels.

She pulls pieces off and feeds them to me with the perfect ratio of warm icing to sweet bread in each bite.

"Delicious," I tell her after she pushes a drop of icing off my lip and onto my tongue.

"Aren't they good?" She moans happily.

"Yeah, the buns are delicious, too." I wink at her and she turns a perfect shade of pink. It matches her top, and her nipples, and all I want for Christmas is a chance to get her alone. Maybe we can sneak off and—

"It's present time for the *grown-ups*," one of the small children hollers. And he shakes a small gold paper box over his head for emphasis.

"That's your present," Rory says, giggling.

"It's not fragile, is it?"

"Not really."

"Listen, I did get you something, but it's more priv—"

"Let's move this nauseating lovefest into the living room," Jules says, bumping into me.

"We're just eating breakfast," Rory protests.

"Finish up, let's go, I got you some good stuff this year."

I catch Rory's wrist, and as soon as everyone has filed into the back room, leaving us alone, I lick her fingers clean. "You go get started. I'm going to catch a shower and get changed."

Since I don't expect any presents other than the one Rory got for me at the last minute, and that the toddler has a good hold on for now, I grab my backpack and head upstairs.

I really do mean to just have a quick shower and head back downstairs.

But then I see Rory's body wash on the ledge, and I think about her little fingers in my mouth.

The next thing I know I've got the bottle uncapped and I'm pouring out just enough that her scent rises around me in the steam.

I brace one hand against the tile and take my cock in hand. Waking up with Rory in my arms two days in a row, and not being able to roll her under me and make her scream is testing all of my resolve.

And she doesn't even know, because she sleeps like a little log.

But she has to know what I was thinking when she was feeding me, right?

Right?

My cock throbs in my grip.

For months, I was so conflicted about hooking up with Rory. On the one hand...I wasn't fucking saying no. On the other, she made it clear she only wanted my cock.

And now that we've been pushed together and forced to work through the point of bristling and barking at each other, and we haven't had sex, I want her even more. On a deeper level.

On a forever level, again.

Not that I ever stopped wanting forever, but it didn't seem like we'd ever be in more than just a holding pattern.

Turns out, I fucking miss what that was, and I got all tangled up in thinking it was a holding pattern.

If that's all that Rory wants, then I'll find a way to be happy as her boyfriend—if she'll have me again.

Chapter 22

Rory

"Bring Uncle Dante another present," my mom says to the twins.

Christmas Day gift opening is a slow process, with the kids bringing my dad each present one at a time. He reads out the label, and then they deliver it to the recipient. None of us exchange many presents anymore, but my sisters and I get each other a little something. This year I got Jules a new pair of headphones, and Cassie a monthly tea subscription.

"This one is for Rory," my dad says.

The twins bring it over, and I glance at the tag. It's not signed, but I recognize the handwriting. "Oh, this one is from Garrett, so I'll wait until he comes downstairs."

I set it behind me, and my dad reads out another name. A present from Tabitha for Allan.

As he opens it, I let my attention drift, and listen to the faint hiss of the shower upstairs. Falling asleep in Garrett's arms last night...something felt different. And then this morning, sharing a cinnamon roll was a lot of fun.

Understatement.

He managed to make something quite innocent downright *filthy*.

I know that fun flirtation doesn't solve whatever failed in our relationship, but it might be a lifeline we can cling to as we sort out the bigger problems.

A quiet giggle behind me is my only clue that one of the twins has stolen Garrett's gift for me before I hear the rip of wrapping paper.

"Hey," I protest, twisting around. "That's mine."

As I say it, I know it's the wrong thing to say to a child. Like a red hot poker to their panic reaction, and wrapping paper goes everywhere as he finishes opening it for me because Christmas is just too exciting.

Jules snags it, her hands crushing the cardboard.

I gasp. "Hey, it might be fragile."

She lifts the lid, frowns, then gets a funny expression on her face. "Nope, not fragile."

Cassie grabs it, but then my mom grabs it before she can look at it.

"Mom, I wouldn't—" Jules starts to say.

"Is it a ring?"

I roll my eyes. "Mom, it's not even ring shaped. Give me my present back, please, before Garrett comes down and sees—"

"I'm here," he says, striding in from the kitchen. His hair is damp, and he's wearing dark jeans and a faded t-shirt in his favourite colour, army green, but this one has some emerald notes, and he looks like a jacked Christmas elf. "What did I miss?"

My mom reaches into the box and holds up a—

A dull buzzing starts in my ears as I immediately recognize the shape of what is in her hand. The length and width and curve and *decoration* of—

"What on earth is this?"

How can she not know?

I'm frozen.

"It's like a tentacle," she says. "It's even got little suckers on it."

I make an inhuman noise as Allan scoops up the toddlers and makes a loud promise of cinnamon buns for them in the kitchen.

"Not a tentacle," Jules chokes out. "More of an eggplant."

My dad mutters something about shovelling the front walk and leaves, not making eye contact with me, my mom, or Garrett, who is a similarly frozen statue of shame in the doorway.

"Eggplants don't have polka dots, though?" My mom sounds so confused, and I can't save her as she taps her index finger against the bright pink bumps that are in the exact same place as Garrett's piercings.

Cassie laughs. "Mom, it's a *dick*."

Mom drops it back into the box, and it starts vibrating. "I don't understand."

Mara snorts. "Carmie, you have three kids and your bed squeaks. Surely you understand."

Garrett clears his throat, and nobody notices except me. He's the last man standing in the room, and it's *his* dick my mom was holding, but all he can do is clear his damn throat?

I glare at him and he shrugs.

Shrugs!

"Turn it off," I mutter.

That, too, goes unnoticed.

Cassie leans over, grabs it, turns it off and waves it in front of my mom's face. "Don't let the purple colour confuse you. This is a dick—"

"Stop saying dick," I yell.

Okay, that was too loud.

"And these are piercings," Cassie continues.

As one, Jules and Mara both swivel their heads to look at Garrett. Not at his ruddy cheeks or his narrowed gaze aimed pointedly at the ceiling, but lower than that.

"Don't look at him," I snap, standing up.

Mara's eyebrows lift as she looks at me. "Is it accurate?"

"Yeah, he's purple," I say sarcastically. "Give me that."

Cassie shakes her head. "Nope. We've scared all the men away. This is a safe space to talk about why Garrett is giving you a dildo."

I choke on a furious, frustrated groan, and swat at her hand. She tosses it to Jules, who climbs up onto the couch, holding it high above my head.

My aunts are dying of laughter.

And Garrett is long gone, the doorway now empty.

My mom looks at me in genuine confusion. "Rory, what was he thinking?"

"What?" I stare back at her. Why is she asking me? I'm not the person who made a purple replica of his cock and then wrapped it in irresistibly shiny paper.

Tabitha wipes her eyes and tries to stop laughing. "Is Garrett...pierced?"

Mara snorts. "Do you really want the answer to that?"

My mom makes a face. "Is this a midlife crisis? It feels a bit young for that."

"Well, he is in love with Rory and that's gotta be hard," Jules adds, very unhelpfully.

"Hey! I'm right here!"

Jules doesn't blink and doesn't look away. "I said what I said. It has to be hard to date you."

"Wow." I jump futilely in the air, then resort to using

my short stature against her and just hook her around the knees, sweeping her legs out from under her.

As I snatch the dildo out of her hands, she gives me the finger with her other hand.

"Real mature," I snap.

"Well," my mother says in her most small town nice lady voice. "I think we can all agree that this is why dickmatized should mean traumatized. Because it just fits."

Chapter 23

Garrett

Rory storms past me in the hallway, double-timing it up the stairs.

I follow, because what the fuck else am I going to do?

"That wasn't supposed to be under the tree—"

"I don't care," she snaps as she reaches the top of the stairs and freezes. "Fuck, I can't even—"

She was heading to her bedroom, I realize, and that's full of Tabitha and Allan's shit.

I take her by the shoulders and guide her down the hall, to a little sitting area outside her parents' bedroom.

It's not private, exactly, but it is more comfortable than the stairs.

And I don't think anyone is going to follow us up here, anyway.

"Roar, I'm sorry." That's a good place to start as I push her into the armchair.

Then I sit on the ottoman and wait for her to say something, anything.

She doesn't. She just stares over my shoulder, a stunned,

humiliated expression on her face. I feel like shit. I did this. I ruined Christmas morning.

And if there was ever an opportunity for Rory's staged breakup, this is it. Fucking hell. It's hard to believe that half an hour ago, I was sucking icing off her fingers and thinking about the future.

"How can I make this right?"

She shakes her head. "It's not something to make right. It's fine. I mean, my mom knows how your cock feels like in her hand now, so that's probably going to be awkward forever for you, and me, but we're all grown-ups."

Right. *Right.* That's the attitude. "Of course."

Her face pinches in tight, her cheeks paling. As if she's just had a painful thought. "I should have just been honest with them from the start."

"You've lost me."

"They all wanted to know why, and I couldn't tell them. I couldn't say anything, because I don't know what you were thinking. My mom asked if this was a mid-life crisis for you."

"No. Jesus, it's... That's not it." I scrub my hands over my face and into my hair. "That was supposed to be a private, funny gift just for you. I don't even know how it ended up under the tree. I'd tucked it beside the couch with my backpack."

She shrugs. "The twins carried it to my dad."

Fuck. When I grabbed my backpack to have my shower, I would have left the gift just laying there, and to a toddler, it looked like fair game. "That's my fault, then."

She drags in a ragged breath. "I don't care about fault. I'm not blaming you. I'm not even mad."

"You're disappointed? Word on the street is that's even worse."

She doesn't laugh.

"Okay, no jokes. Now isn't the time—"

"Why *did* you make it?" She lifts her gaze and frowns at me. "And when? Because this—" she wiggles the dildo between us. "This doesn't happen overnight, right?"

I wince. "No, not overnight."

"So what exactly is this?"

I take a deep breath. "I had it made in the summer." I glance at the open hallway behind me and lower my voice. "After the second time we hooked up. You were conflicted about it, and I didn't know how I felt about it, either. And I saw an ad. It felt like..."

"Like what?"

"It was the only thing you liked about me, Roar. I thought it would be cleaner if I just...gave it to you."

"You were going to break up with me." She sounds so indignant.

"We were already broken up. I can't do that twice." Except now it feels like we're on a collision course for me to do exactly that, and I feel sick over it.

"But this was a going away present?"

"I don't know. I wouldn't call it that."

"What would you call it?"

"A funny joke."

"It doesn't feel funny." Bright tears threaten to spill from her lovely, furious eyes. She swipes at them, her fingers shaking.

I reach out and catch her hands and take a deep breath. "I'm sorry. I see that now. I shouldn't have brought it. I was torn. I didn't know when or how—"

"But you did bring it. Like two days ago, you thought you should give me that, and then I wouldn't need you anymore? Is that right?"

When I don't answer her, because yes, that's right, even though it feels very, very wrong, she nods her head firmly.

"Got it. You wormed your way back into my heart—"

"Wormed?"

"—and the whole time you were going to give me this replacement dick and move on?"

"Not the whole time. That's not how I felt this morning. Roar, I want a second chance with you."

She stares at me, stunned. "What?"

"The last two days have changed everything. I think you feel it, too. I know we have a lot to talk about still, but I want to put the work in. I want to find a way back to being happy together."

She looks at the dildo in her hand, then back at me. "What about the ninety-minute rule?"

"Yeah, we still seem to fight every hour and a half. But we're pushing through it, aren't we? I can handle you being mad at me. Anything is better than the freeze out."

She shakes her head. "No."

"Why not?"

"Because...." She cuts off a sob and shoves the stupid purple sex toy at me. "I deserve more than tolerance. I missed *you* when I texted you in the summer, you dummy. Not your dick. But you hate my job so much, you couldn't even see that. You just—"

"I don't hate your job."

"Yes, you do." She pushes out of the chair, her small body slipping past me.

Slipping away, again.

I catch her by the wrist and tug her back, sprawling her across my lap. "Don't run away."

She shoves at my chest.

I catch her wrists and hold her palms to my body. "Don't. Run. Away."

"I'm not *running*," she protests, her eyes wild. "I'm just *done*."

There's a footstep on the stairs, and I know we have an audience. I don't know if it's her mother, or her sisters, or tiny children, but we're no longer alone.

Damn it all to hell.

"I know you're done," I say quietly, my heart breaking. "But I also know you're miserable and it's not because of me."

"What the hell does that mean?"

"I don't hate your job, Roar." Fuck. *Fuck.* I take a deep breath. "*You* hate your job."

Chapter 24

Rory

I scramble off Garrett's lap, but before I can yell at him because *what the fuck do you mean*, my mom appears at the top of the stairs.

My pulse is pounding and I can't get it under control.

"Rory," my mom says, and something in her voice cuts through the red haze.

I blink and refocus on her worried face.

Garrett stands, too.

"Jake called. Something's wrong with Dani."

The drive to the hospital is completely silent.

I don't argue with Garrett that he should drive. He can't exactly stay at the farm with my aunts and sisters, and I don't have a vehicle, even if I did want to drive myself, which I don't.

I'm still shaking when he pulls up in front of the entrance.

"Go on in and find her," he says. "I'll park."

I find my cousin in a bed in Emergency.

"Hey," I say softly as I slide around the curtain.

Jake looks up from where he had his head bowed over her hand.

Dani gives me a weak smile. "Hi. Sorry to drag you away from Christmas morning."

"Oh." I let out a watery laugh. "Yeah, that was already ruined. Don't worry. What's going on?"

"She woke up bleeding this morning," Jake says.

"I know it can be normal," Dani adds. "But this wasn't normal."

I squeeze her hand. "You did the right thing coming in. They're going to run some tests and do some imaging, and I'll stay with you the whole time."

"Thank you." She closes her eyes and takes a deep breath. "How was your Christmas morning ruined?"

"I don't want to make you laugh right now. And it's also embarrassing and I don't want to look at Jake when I'm telling you."

Her eyebrows curve up. "Oh?"

Her husband pats her shoulder. "That's my sign to go call the kids."

I circle around to sit in the chair he vacates. "Okay, I'm going to tell you something but I'm swearing you to secrecy for now."

Dani nods. "My lips are sealed. Please distract me."

"Garrett and I broke up in April."

She stares at me. "What?"

"Yeah."

"But you're...."

I shrug. "I know. It's a long story that starts and ends with I'm a hot mess who can't do much right, besides being a doctor, and um...I don't actually love being a doctor. Apparently."

Her brows knit together hard. "What???"

"That's what Garrett says. He says I hate my job, and it ruined our relationship, and then we hooked up a few times —" I cut myself off. "I'm telling this very badly."

"Oh, no, now you're getting to the good stuff. So you're back together?"

"Definitely not."

"So you're exes with benefits?"

I squirm. "Yeah. We were. Now... Now I don't think we're anything. Not after this morning."

"What happened this morning?"

"Tabitha's boys accidentally opened a present Garrett got for me. A *private* present." I grimace. "A replica dildo of, and I quote, *the only part of his body that I seem to like.*"

"He said that?"

"Something like that. It might be a paraphrase."

"Wow." Dani shakes her head. "I mean, I love Jake with my whole heart, but sometimes that part of him can really save the day, you know? It's sort of a compliment."

"We're not at the *taking it like a compliment* stage right now." I roll my shoulders, trying to shake the tension there. "And the worst part is that he's right. The first time he came over after we broke up, I basically demanded that we...." I lower my voice. "You know."

She laughs gently. "Yes, I know. Do you know, Dr. Minelli?"

"I barely recognized myself."

"So it was good sex?"

"It was *great* sex. The best ever, and we'd always had good sex."

"But then it got complicated."

"Yeah. So he made a replica, and then...." I tell her the whole story. About buying a car that turned out to be crap, about Garrett coming to the rescue, and his ninety-minute limit, and how we blew that out of the water with a road trip, and we survived. But just barely. "And the worst part is that we've been so close the last two days. Like it's been..." I shiver. "Really nice. Except the whole time, he had this *gift*, and then... Now my entire family has an eggplant emoji vision of what his—"

The curtain pulls back, and the rest of that sentence gets strangled in my throat.

"I'm Dr. Schmidt." Under the embroidered name on his white coat it reads *Chief of Obstetrics*, so either this guy is single and doesn't care about Christmas, or his department is understaffed if he's pulling holiday shifts himself. "I understand you're thirteen weeks pregnant? And you woke up to significant, spontaneous bleeding?"

"That's right." Dani runs through her own vitals. "I'm a paramedic."

"You're being a better patient than most health workers," Dr. Schmidt says. "I want to do an ultrasound to start."

"This is my cousin." Dani gestures to me.

"Rory Minelli," I say, introducing myself. "I'm an OB/GYN PGY5 in Ottawa."

"All right, then. Welcome to an impromptu ultrasound clinic, Dr. Minelli. Your cousin doesn't mind including you in this?"

"No, I want her to be here," Dani says.

"Of course. Let's take a look and see if we can figure out what's going on." He adjusts the sheet covering her down to her hips, then folds up her hospital gown, revealing a slight swell.

Jake returns as Dr. Schmidt is spreading gel on Dani's belly.

"He's just taking a look," she whispers.

They lock hands together, and I turn my attention to the ultrasound screen to give them some privacy in what has to be an agonizing moment.

The flicker of a fetus moving is immediately obvious. "There's a strong heartbeat," Dr. Schmidt says.

Jake and Dani exhale as one.

I grip the plastic footboard, because I know they aren't out of the woods yet, but that's phenomenal news.

He shifts his angle, getting us a different view of her uterus. "Do you have any pain, Dani?"

"No."

"And no history of premature delivery in your other pregnancies?"

"None."

He glances back at me, and I know that look. It's a test, a consultant giving a resident a split second to read their mind.

"And you had vaginal deliveries with the other three kids?" I ask.

"Yes, I've been blessed with easy pregnancies and deliveries." Dani glances back and forth between us. "What do you see?"

He shifts the angle again, bringing the placenta into view—right above her cervix. "Your placenta has attached lower in your uterus this time. It's a condition called placenta previa. It's a common cause of second trimester bleeding. We're going to want to keep you here until the bleeding resolves, and you'll need to be on bed rest when you go home."

"I have three kids. And a job." Dani looks at me. "This will resolve, right?"

"Dr. Schmidt will follow you closely, but the best thing you can do to protect this pregnancy is let Jake worry about the kids."

"On it," he says. "She won't move a muscle."

Dr. Schmidt cleans up her belly, then stands up. "I'll go find out if we can get you moved to the antenatal ward for the night. Hopefully you'll get to go home tomorrow."

I follow him out to the nurse station. "Can I be an obnoxious resident and ask a follow up question?"

He laughs. "Sure."

"Would you consider doing a cerclage?"

"Are they teaching you to do unnecessary procedures on family members in Ottawa, Dr. Minelli?"

"I know the literature doesn't support it as an intervention for previa, but there are a couple of things that stand out to me as unusual. She's having this bleeding earlier than many do. It's her fourth pregnancy, which means her cervix is already primed to dilate. And even if it doesn't help, the procedure itself is minimally invasive. Unnecessary, maybe. Safe, yes. Why not try? And if it does help, then it's worth writing up in a paper."

"You had me until the last part. Don't make more work for me. If I wanted to write papers, I'd work at a big city hospital like you do." He says it kindly. He picks up the phone and calls upstairs. "I need to admit a patient for observation. And we might need to book the procedure room for—" He moves the phone away from his mouth. "Does tomorrow work for you to observe?"

I blink in surprise. "You'd let me scrub in?"

"You've probably placed more cerclages than I have in the last year. You might as well talk me through it."

"Tomorrow's fine. Great. Thank you." I grin at him. "I won't be obnoxious."

"We'll get her moved upstairs, and then I'll do an internal exam before the end of my shift tonight. And in the meantime, I want you to send me whatever literature you think might back up your case." He pauses. "You didn't have any other plans for Christmas Day, did you?"

My answer is immediate and sincere. "Not at all."

Chapter 25

Garrett

I'm sitting in the waiting room, thinking about going in search of a coffee, when I get a text message from my cousin Owen, who I saw briefly yesterday when I dropped off presents for his kids.

OWEN

Hey bud, are you around today?

GARRETT

I might be later. Currently in town with Rory.

In town means any town bigger than Pine Harbour. It means off the peninsula, running an errand or shopping or doing something important. And that's as specific as I'm going to get right now.

OWEN

When you get back, come by my place. I have an interesting surprise for you.

I drop a thumbs up on that, and then go back to bouncing my leg nervously.

189

I'm just about to text Rory and let her know I'm going to find out if the cafeteria is open on Christmas Day when she pushes through the waiting room door and rushes to my side.

"Hi," she says breathlessly, as if the last thing she didn't pretty much say to me was that we were done. Or *she* was done, which is the same thing.

"Hi," I say back guardedly. "How's Dani?"

"She's being admitted, but there's a good fetal heartbeat. Listen, I'm going to stay here for the rest of the day. And I need to be here tomorrow, too, so I might just crash in one of the on-call rooms."

I stare at her.

"What?" She brushes a wild curl off her forehead.

"Rory, it's Christmas and you're on vacation."

"Dani needs me."

"She needs you to sleep in an on-call room?"

"No, but I need to do some research—"

I hold up my hand, cutting her off. Standing, I gesture for her to follow me.

At least she actually does follow, that's something. We step outside. It's started snowing, finally. Fat, wet flakes float lazily to the sidewalk, but where we're standing under the overhang, it's not too cold.

I search her face. She stares back at me, wild-eyed.

"What research do you need to do?"

"The OB on call was open to a suggestion of mine, but he wants me to back it up." She juts her chin up. "And I want to do that."

"You do." When she doesn't say anything, I laugh under my breath. "Got it. Research is easier than going back to face your mom and deal with the fact that she heard us break up again. What do you want me to do, pack up your things? Deal with Carmen and Dante? Say my goodbyes and then just wait in the parking lot here until you're done playing The Good Doctor and we can drive back to Ottawa in stony silence?"

It all comes pouring out of me.

Fucking fuck.

She stares at me, her eyes narrowing, turning steely and determined instead of wild and desperate. Nothing like a good rage to focus Dr. Aurora Minelli.

"Sure, make me the bad guy, Garrett. Couldn't ever be you. Couldn't ever be Mr. Tells Himself a Story So He Doesn't Need to Communicate."

"What story do I tell myself?"

"That I hate my job."

Ah. I guess we're doing this now. That's what the angry jut of her chin is all about.

"I *don't* hate my job," she repeats, as if it wasn't fucking obvious that's her opinion. "You shouldn't have said that."

"No? Why not? Did it hit too close to home? And now you're...what, working pro bono on your cousin's case to prove that point? You love being a doctor so much you'll leap at the first opportunity?"

"I'm just *observing*," she snaps. "It's an interesting case."

"It's your *cousin*! Don't you think for a second you should just feel something here? Worry?"

"Of course I'm worried! I'm not going to actually treat her. I'm just talking to her physician."

"Instead of talking to your mother."

"Whoa. Offside. And have you tried talking to my mother? She'll just find a way to spin it to where I should be grateful to you for giving me a parting gift."

"This is good, Roar. Get it all out. Tell me how much

you hate the—" The door opens and an elderly couple comes out, moving slowly.

Rory grabs my arm and pulls me around the corner, to the empty ambulance bay. I think she means for us to keep arguing, but as soon as her back collides with the concrete wall, my hands are in her hair, holding her head, and my mouth is on hers.

She tastes like adrenalin and too-sweet coffee. She kisses me back like she's fucking mad that we don't kiss more often, and I share that bittersweet opinion.

I drag her up against my body, filling my arms with all of her fight. She sinks her fingers into my hair, making little fists, and I don't think she realizes just how tight she's holding on to me as she kisses me back with everything she has.

I love you, you hellion, I want to say. But she doesn't want to hear that.

Instead, I let her take what she needs from me, and when she finally sags back, I hold her close and just keep breathing.

"If you want to stay here and do research," I finally whisper. "Stay and do that. I could go have some Kincaid family time anyway. My cousin texted me. But I'll drive back down and collect you tonight."

"You don't need to do that."

But I want to. I *need* to. "We have two more nights, Rory. I want to spend them together."

I'm not going to get another chance at these last moments of *us*. I know how I fucked things up the first time, by letting her retreat. No more of that.

Her fingers tighten on my jacket. "Weather is rolling in."

"Weather is always rolling in. And sometimes it actually

does. But I've got big tires on my truck, and I'm not letting you sleep in an on-call room unless Dani's life literally depends on it."

She's forced to admit that it does not.

I kiss her again, and send her back inside.

Then I hit the highway and head north.

There's a pile of cars in front of my cousin's place when I pull up. We've never done Christmas together, except one year when I was a young teenager and my dad was in the hospital. Owen had a young daughter at the time, and his brothers were all young adults. I was an awkward in between age, and an extra burden on a stressed single dad.

Now that daughter, Becca, is all grown up, and she has a little boy with her high school boyfriend, who now plays pro hockey. And Owen is remarried, and he has two little girls with his new wife. Most of his brothers have kids now, too.

And once again, I'm the odd guy out, stuck in between the generations.

But I trudge up his walk anyway, because the other two options—staying at the hospital all day, or going back to the tree farm—are even less appealing right now.

At least nobody here has talked about my dick so far today.

Of course, it is Pine Harbour, and the day is not over.

I knock at the door, and it opens immediately.

A large man in a cowboy hat gives me a big grin. "Is this Garrett?"

"It is," I say cautiously, glancing past him.

The living room is *full* of Kincaids. Every brother waves back at me, and a bunch of kids are playing on the floor in between them.

"I'm Zane." He grins, like he's barely containing the punchline to a joke. "Zane Kincaid."

Four hours later, I pull my truck to a stop in front of Rory's parents' house.

I turn off the engine, but I don't get out right away.

I'm *reeling*.

Part of me wants to still be at Owen's place, learning everything I can about Zane and his brothers and their mother.

I have an aunt.

Holy fuck.

Life hasn't been easy for her, and we're going to have to take it slow, but...I have a whole other side of my family that I had no clue about.

My heart hurts as I think about my dad, and the grief he never got out from under about his sister running away from home as a teenager.

There's a rap at my passenger side window, making me jump.

Cassie opens the door and climbs up.

"I'm coming in," I say. "Rory's at the hospital. She's, uh, throwing herself into making sure Dani has the best obstetrical care possible."

"Maybe she should stay there," Cass mutters.

"Oh, no." I gesture to the key. "Should I start this thing up? Make a great escape?"

She shakes her head—but then bursts into tears.

Fucking hell. I find some Tim Horton's napkins, which don't really help that much, but they're possibly better than nothing. "What's going on?"

"Are you and Rory breaking up?"

I close my eyes and exhale. "It's complicated."

"I don't recommend a Christmas breakup."

"How are you doing?"

"Terribly. I miss Nate."

"Have you talked to him?"

"We've texted a little."

"That's good."

"Is it?" She shrugs and hunkers down in her coat. "I want to move back home and make him move out."

"You need help with that?"

She shakes her head. "He's agreed."

"Okay, good."

"I can't live with my parents, you know?"

"Yeah."

"I love them."

"Of course. We all love them."

"Rory's better with the boundaries."

I laugh. "Maybe too much for her own good, though."

"What does that mean?"

I sigh. "Let's go inside."

The kids are nowhere to be heard, and Allan is missing, too, so hopefully they're napping, because Carmen is standing at the sink with red-rimmed eyes and a dish towel twisted in her hands. Tabitha and Mara are at the table, and everyone falls silent as soon as I step into the kitchen.

Crap.

Behind me, Cassie slinks past us and disappears up the stairs, but there's furious whispering, and she quickly returns with Jules.

The silence stretches uncomfortably. No one's looking at me directly, which means they're all thinking about this morning.

"So I guess we should talk about it," I say.

Carmen's face turns neon pink. "We don't need to."

"Actually, we do." I cross my arms. "Let's just get it out there. That was awkward, right? Slightly embarrassing for me that you all know more about my anatomy than I thought you ever would. But it was mortifying for Rory."

The silence that follows is telling.

"Most of the blame for that obviously lies with me. I thought—wrongly—that it would be a private gift between Rory and myself. My mistake was amplified by the teasing, though. Were you all oblivious to her distress?"

Mara looks at Tabitha, uneasy.

So maybe not completely oblivious.

"She doesn't want to come back. She will, and she'll put on a brave face, but that's not the holiday that she wanted, and I don't think it's the holiday any of you wanted, either."

Carmen looks genuinely confused. "What would she rather do?"

"Stay at the hospital. She threatened to sleep in an on-call room."

"Is she allowed to do that?" Cassie asks.

"Can you imagine trying to tell her no?" Jules mutters.

Mara nods, though. "Let me guess. The hospital is the only place she feels like she's good enough right now?"

I nod grimly.

"We weren't trying to—" Carmen starts. Then she

stops. And she makes a fluttery motion with her hands, and lets out a watery cry. "That silly girl."

Dante comes in from the back room. "What's this all about? Oh. Garrett."

That's a significantly colder tone than asking me yesterday if I wanted money for a diamond ring. Which is what I get for giving his daughter a customized vibrating eggplant in my likeness.

"Garrett is worried about Rory," Carmen says to her husband. "He says she's hiding at the hospital."

"That's *not* what I said." But I could just as easily have said the same thing to Rory. Guilt churns in my belly. "Rory will come home tonight because she puts holding this family together above all else, including her own happiness. Ask yourselves, why does she have to be the one to do that?"

She blinks in surprise.

"You trying to make a point, son?" Dante grunts.

Definitely mad about the dildo.

Only way to get through it is to go *through* it, though. "At some point soon, Rory might make some choices that you don't understand. And when she does, I want you all to support her no matter what."

"Of course we will," Dante says.

Except no, he might not. That's not a given.

"We just want her to be happy," Carmen adds.

"Do you? Or do you want her to seem happy no matter what?" I push off from the counter. "You guys need to step up and carry some of the happiness responsibility."

They all just stare at me.

In for a penny, in for a pound. Might as well go all in. I look at Rory's father. "Sir, can we talk in private?"

He looks startled. "Yes, I suppose. If everything is all right here?"

Carmen waves us on. "Go. I'm sure Cassie and Jules can pick up where Garrett left off."

He looks like he doesn't want to know what that means, and that's for the best. He grunts and nods at me. "I was going to spray down the skating trail. Come with me."

As we walk down the lane to the tree lot, the fresh snow squeaking under our boots, I try to order my thoughts.

"Well, out with it," he finally says, impatiently.

"I'm not sure where to start."

"Garrett, son, I've known you for nearly fifteen years. You've been in love with my daughter every second of that time. Whatever it is, I can handle it, even if I don't like it. You've always been good to Rory—"

"That's the thing. I haven't."

He turns on me, his hands immediately curling into fists. Can't blame it. That sounded ominous.

I hold up my own hands. "I've never cheated on her. Don't look at me like that."

"Then what?"

"Earlier this year, I lost sight of...us. We've been struggling ever since. I don't want to say more than that, because it's private, and Rory doesn't know I'm telling you this. But last night, when you joked to her that she might lose me, that pressed on a very sensitive bruise. One that I gave her, unfortunately."

"Ah, fuck."

"Yeah."

"Why the fuck didn't you say something?"

"I don't know."

"Jesus, kid. Now I'm the asshole." He makes a face. "You could have ripped me for that in front of the girls, you know."

I shake my head. "I don't want them to know that we're rocky. Not if Rory doesn't want to tell anyone."

"All right. Your secret is safe with me. But you fix this, yeah? You make it right with her?"

"Yeah, I'm going to try."

"Don't try. Do."

"Easier said than done." I shake my head. "Look, loving Rory is hard, because deep down, Rory doesn't trust that she's loveable. And I think—I know your family is close. Your house is chaos at the holidays. So much love, right? But there are strings attached to that love, and that scares her."

He scoffs.

This is the hard part. "Dante, you don't speak to your brother."

He falls silent.

I switch gears before he gets mad and tells me to mind my own fucking business. "Did you ever know my father's sister?"

Warily, he shakes his head. "I don't think so. She ran away as a teenager? I think that was before we moved here. Very sad, very sad."

"Well, it turns out, she's alive and living in Alberta. She's good now, but she was in a controlling relationship for a long time. She has four sons. They're right around my age. I met one of them today."

"What?" He claps me on the shoulder. "Garrett, that's wonderful news."

"It is. But I wish my dad was here to be reconnected with them, you know?"

He takes a deep breath, his eyes closing, and he nods. "I understand."

I hope he does. Because I'm not going to let anyone tell

Rory that she might lose me if she's not enough. She will always be enough for me.

Chapter 26

Rory

"You're hot shit."

I jerk my head up and see that I'm not alone in the small resident room. Based on the schedule posted on the wall, there are a couple of surgical residents here, doing rural rotations, but neither of them are actually *in* the hospital today, and one of the nurses said I could use the computer.

Dr. Schmidt has tracked me down, apparently.

"I'm a good doctor."

"That's an understatement. You're chief resident at one of the busiest OB/GYN programs in the country."

I shrug. "Must be a quiet day here if you're looking into me."

"My wife went on a cruise with her parents. I don't have anything else to do today."

"Oh." I wince. "Sorry."

"Don't be. I'm glad I was here when Dani came in, and I'm glad I got to meet you. Turns out I went to school with your program director."

I don't mind that he was checking up on me—I stormed

into his hospital and started suggesting shit—but something about the way he drops Glenda's name makes me feel vaguely queasy. "Oh? That's a small world."

"Relax, it's fine." He gestures to the chair next to mine. "Can I sit?"

"It's your hospital."

"Yeah." He sprawls out and pulls off his surgical cap. Under it he's got more grey hair than I expected. His face is relatively youthful. "What are your plans for next year?"

The queasiness intensifies. I hear Garrett's voice echoing from earlier. *I don't hate your job, Roar. You* hate *your job.* I force the gross, slimy feeling down and reach for the same answer I've been giving the surgeons in my program for months. "I'm still exploring my options."

"Are you leaning towards a fellowship? Or do you want to go straight to a consultant position?"

Since he's clearly talked about this with my program director, and probably knows I haven't done any job interviews yet, I admit the most sanitized version of the truth. "I'm behind on that process."

To my surprise, he just shrugs. "You'll find something. And there's always locums."

I stare at him.

He laughs. "What, you thought I'd give you a hard time?" He shakes his head. "You've been beating yourself up about this for months, I bet. I don't need to pile on top of that."

I let out a shaky exhale. "Thanks."

He clicks his tongue against his teeth and pushes to his feet. "I saw the lit review you sent me, and I agree that the risks are minimal. I'm not going to do an internal exam today, we'll just see what her cervix looks like tomorrow."

I jump up. "Are you going to tell her now?"

"You want to come with me?"

"Of course." I grab my purse and coat, and chase after him.

When we get to Dani's room on the antenatal floor, she has company—Garrett's cousin's wife, Kerry, who is a midwife.

She lights up when she sees me. "Have you talked to Garrett yet?"

Confused, I shake my head. "No. Why?"

She mimes zipping her lips. "His story to tell." Then she gives Dr. Schmidt a friendly smile. "Dani says she was in good hands earlier."

He glances my way, his expression amused. "She really was. Dr. Minelli, why don't you explain your thought process? And then we'll discuss next steps."

I step forward and slide right through all the relevant details. I go over why I think Dani's an exception to the standard protocol, and what the risks and potential benefits might be. Kerry asks pointed questions, because as a midwife her model of care is based on more comprehensive informed choice, a step beyond the informed consent standard in medicine. By the time I see a patient, there's usually one clear path, and we take it as efficiently as possible to get the safest, best outcomes possible.

But on this quiet Christmas Day, as snow pelts at the window, with a patient who is like a big sister to me, who is a medical professional herself, it's special to be able to not just give the highlights and my evidence-based medical opinion about the obvious path to take.

Dani and Kerry ask pointed questions about the procedure, and they talk out what a lower-intervention path might be.

I know this isn't what it would be like to practice medicine here all the time. There's nothing routine about this moment.

But when we finally decide that yes, we'll go ahead tomorrow with an examination and a probable cerclage, for exceptional reasons, I'm filled with a curious lightness.

Chapter 27

Garrett

I text Rory when I get to the hospital, but she doesn't reply immediately, so I pay for parking and head inside.

I run into Owen's wife, Kerry, at the elevators.

"Garrett!" She gives me a hug. "Nice to see you twice in one day. I just left Dani. She's in good hands with Rory and Aiden."

"Aiden?"

"Aiden Schmidt. Head of obstetrics here. Happened to be on call today."

I nod, but a weird tension coils at the base of my neck. "Are they still busy with Dani?"

"I don't think so. You can head up and collect your girl." She waves good night as she heads for the door. "See you tomorrow!"

Right. Cousin lunch at the diner.

The elevator doors are slow to close, and the button takes forever to light up even after I press it twice.

Time silently ticks by in pulse-thudding seconds. The car creaks to life and starts to rise.

Rory and Aiden.

It's completely irrational, I know that, but even before the elevator doors open, I know I'm going to be jealous of this guy who Rory chose to spend Christmas Day with, because she's so fucking desperate to prove that she doesn't hate her job.

Why the fuck did I say that to her?

With everything else that's happened today, I'd shoved the mental replay of our fight this morning to the back of my mind, but it all comes raging back when I turn the corner and see Rory with her elbows on the nurse's station outside Dani's room, a tall silver-haired man in scrubs and a white lab coat leaning over her.

Both of them laughing.

I don't hate my job. You shouldn't have said that.

No fucking shit. I sent her running right back to it.

And as I stride toward them, it gets even worse.

"Why, are you going to offer me a job?" she teases.

He grins. "Is that an option?"

She shakes her head. "No." Then she catches sight of me, and her eyes go wide. "Garrett, hi."

The doc holds out his hand and gives me an easy smile. "Aiden Schmidt."

Don't crush his hand in your fist, I think as I shake his hand. I manage to stay civilized. "Garrett Kincaid."

"Ah, yes. A Kincaid, of course. Nice to meet you." Then he taps the counter right next to Rory's elbow. "See you tomorrow. I'm assuming you'll barge in on rounds, too?"

"For sure. I want to hear how that breech delivery goes." Her eyes are fucking twinkling as she waves goodbye, then turns to me. "Dani's asleep, if you were hoping to see her."

I shake my head. *I only wanted to see you,* I could say. It would be the fucking truth. But I don't make her eyes light up the way work does, so I keep that to myself. "It's fine. Your mom's got Christmas dinner in a holding pattern back at the farm."

Her face pinches tight, all the joy disappearing in an instant.

"I, um, talked to them. About this morning. We cleared the air on it being awkward, so nobody's going to bother you about it when we get there."

She snorts. "Sure."

"No, for real." I hunch my shoulders up and shove my hands in my pockets to keep from grabbing her. "I know you don't want to come home tonight. Or at least, I know it's complicated. Everyone is hard on you, and nobody listens. Including me."

"Not including you." She lifts her hand, then tentatively reaches for me, sliding her fingers into the open gap of my unzipped coat. "You see me, and hear me, even when I don't hear myself."

The relief I feel when she closes her hand around the front of my shirt is enough to bring me to my knees.

"I don't know about that," I manage to say. "I saw how happy you were when I stepped off that elevator."

A flare of surprise flashes across her face, followed immediately by her brows pulling in. "What did you see?"

I glance around. We're all alone. But this is hardly private.

"It's okay," she whispers. "I want to know how you see me."

"You were relaxed, and joking." I swallow hard. "And I had a beat of irrational jealousy. I love hearing you laugh, do you know that?"

She tips her head to the side, her gaze fixed on my face. "You make me laugh."

"I haven't for a long time. I mostly just make you mad."

She huffs a little chuckle under her breath. Not the kind of laugh I meant, but I'll take it. "Yeah, well, that might be true sometimes, but it's not true all the time. And there's zero need for you to be jealous."

Pushing up on her toes, her hand tightens in my shirt, and she tugs me down towards her.

"I'm sorry about fighting this morning," she whispers before she brushes her lips against mine.

Her kiss is soft and sweet and chaste, but it's enough to make my head spin. I groan her name against her lips, then finally give in to my desperate desire to put my arms around her.

"I hate fighting," I whisper against her hair. "And I'm sorry for the boneheaded present."

She takes a deep breath, then lets it out. "I told Dani about it. She called me a prude."

"You're not a prude." I laugh softly. "You're a little she-devil when you want to be. And I—" *I love you for it.*

But I cut myself off.

"Come on, let me take you home. I have something really wild to tell you."

She tucks in under my arm. "Kerry said there was something, but she refused to spill the details."

That puts the *A Kincaid, of course* into some context, I suppose. "So I went to Owen's place this afternoon, and this big, brawny cowboy answered the door. Introduces himself as Zane. Zane Kincaid. It turns out, we have a whole branch of the family out west."

"What?" She stops and stares at me. "How?"

"It's a really long story, and he says a lot of it isn't his to share, not yet. But my dad's sister is alive and well, and has four grown boys."

"And they all have her name?"

"Now they do, yeah. They grew up with a different name, but their father was an abusive piece of shit, and as adults, they all took her name."

"Oh my God." She throws her arms around me and gives me a tight squeeze. "That must have been so intense to learn."

"Rocked my world, that's for sure."

She guides me into a nook halfway down the hall and gently presses me against the wall. "Was it just him?"

I sag back, nodding. "He's taken the lead. He found Owen, and they connected a month ago. He flew out to surprise everyone today, and we're going to organize a trip out West to meet our aunt at some point soon."

"Wow." She searches my face. "How do you feel?"

"Overwhelmed."

"Of course."

"It, um..." I swallow around an unexpected lump in my throat.

"Yeah." She steps in close and leans against me, giving me her warm little weight.

I close my eyes and lower my head to rest my cheek on the top of hers.

"I wish my dad was still alive," I manage to get out.

"Me, too," she whispers back.

"This morning feels like so long ago."

She exhales slowly. "It really does."

"I need to tell you something." I wrap my arms around her in case she wants to bolt. I'm not letting her do that. "I told your dad that we've been struggling since the spring. I needed him to know that when he told you that you might lose me, that was pushing on a bruise."

"Oh."

"I told him in private. And it's a variation on the truth, in a way."

"I told Dani the whole truth."

I shift so I can see her face. "You did?"

She nods, her eyes darting as she searches for my reaction.

Both of us uncertain. But oddly on the same page. It's a good feeling.

"That's good." I take a deep breath. "I wasn't sure if you'd want to."

"You tried to tell me that it would be okay."

"You were scared. I get it."

"I'll tell my family, too. As soon as we get back."

That makes me laugh.

"What?"

"I just yelled at them all to not let anything touch the sacredness of Christmas Dinner for you, and you're going to race in like a wrecking ball." I catch her chin and stop her from protesting. "A beautiful, perfect wrecking ball. Let's go tell them that we broke up. But we're also going to tell them that we're working out our differences and they shouldn't be surprised if they find us sleeping on the same couch tomorrow morning."

Her eyebrows lift, and her cheeks pink with pleasure. "Are we working out our differences? I thought you ordered me a detachable version of your cock because we needed a clean break?"

I groan. "I was too hasty in thinking that."

"We can't continue like we were."

"We won't." I kiss the tip of her nose, then lift her face

another inch so I can cover her lips with mine. "We're going to keep talking. And we aren't going to stop until we get it right this time. So you can tell them when we get back to the farm, or later, if you want. It's Christmas, Rory. All I want for the last few hours of the holiday is for you to be genuinely happy."

Chapter 28

Rory

I don't tell them.

It's not the coward's way out, I justify to myself. When we get back to the farm, there's a thick white blanket of snow everywhere, but my whole family spills out onto the porch anyway. And they are earnest and sweet.

"How's Dani?" asks Cassie.

"Are you hungry?" asks my mom.

And Jules makes it clear that she values me deeply. "Thank God you're back, we need a fourth for euchre."

Garrett wraps his arm around my waist and kisses my temple. "Dinner first, then a savage card game?"

"Sounds perfect," I whisper.

And it is.

"Mara made us all Christmas crackers," Aunt Tabitha says as I'm ushered into the dining room.

So before we dig in to the feast, we take turns making them pop with the people who sit beside us. Instead of the paper crown and a plastic toy that would be in the usual crackers from the store, there are delicate twisted wire crowns threaded with tiny, glittering beads, and hand lettered knock knock jokes that make everyone groan.

"Knock knock," Mom says to Dad.

"Who's there?"

"Anna."

"Anna who?"

"Anna partridge in a pear tree."

Garrett glances at his. "I think I'm next." He clears his throat and looks at me. "Knock knock."

"Who's there?"

"Tuta."

I shake my head, already laughing. "Tuta who?"

"Two turtle doves."

My mom and dad look at each other and then say in unison, "And a partridge in a pear tree."

So it goes around the table, everyone figuring out which groaner pun goes next. Some are terrible—*Thor, Thor who? Thor E. Frenchens*—and some are corny—*Fork, Fork who, Fork Awling Birds*. But they all make us laugh, and after each punchline, we sing the rest of the song as a group.

When we get to five golden rings each time, there's a tiny twinge of regret deep in my belly, but with Garrett's warm, muscular thigh pressed against my leg and his arm slung casually around the back of my chair, I can't feel sorry for myself.

We may have bruised each other a lot this year, a real struggle as he told my dad, but somehow we're ending the year together again, if in the most tentative, feeling-it-out kind of way.

Dinner is slow and indulgent. My mom has outdone herself, with raisin studded sausage and onion stuffing, orange and cranberry relish, green bean casserole, butternut squash, roasted beets, and a golden turkey that tastes like heaven.

My dad serves a nice bottle of wine, coming around the table to fill everyone's glass himself. When he gets to me, he kisses the top of my head and pats Garrett on the shoulder. "I'm glad this one went out in the snow to bring you home."

"More than once," I murmur. And then I hold Garrett's gaze as my dad moves on. The depth of feeling in his eyes tells me that he's also thinking of the other morning. "I'm glad you came to find me."

"Always," he says, and it feels like a promise that I can believe with surprising ease.

After a bottle of ice wine, a tray of toddler-decorated Christmas cookies, and five brutal games of euchre, my family slowly heads upstairs to bed, and Garrett and I finally have the back room to ourselves.

After we take turns in the bathroom and I take my pill with a quick gulp of water in the kitchen, Garrett turns out all the lights—except the ones on the tree.

He's wearing his comfy clothes from last night, soft sweatpants and a faded t-shirt. I'm wearing long johns and a t-shirt, nothing underneath. Very ordinary clothes, nothing sexy per se, but there's a quiet arc of electricity in the air.

"Not to bring up the unfortunate topic of Christmas presents again," he says. "But I noticed there's still a gift under the tree with my name on it."

I gasp and race to find it.

"I can't believe I forgot." I hand it over. "And it might be the wine talking, but I've been thinking more about the... you know."

His mouth curves up in a slow, sexy smile. "Dildo."

My tummy quivers. "Yes."

He stretches out on the couch, his gift unopened in his hands. "What have you been thinking?"

"If it had been a private gift...if I'd opened it now, when everyone is asleep upstairs...and you'd had a chance to explain why you were giving it to me..."

"That's a lot of conditions."

"But they're important, because I know that's what you intended."

"I don't know. I think no matter what, it would have pushed on some bruises that I wasn't seeing."

I blink, surprised. Not at the thoughtfulness of it— Garrett has shown me a lot of that kind of careful kindness the last few days. But I'm genuinely surprised that he thinks he *didn't* see something in me.

"What kind of bruises?" I ask, and then wave my hands. "Wait. Wait. Open your present. They might be related, in a way."

His eyebrows shoot up. "Oh?"

"Tangentially."

He rips away the ribbon and paper, then turns the timer over in his hands. It doesn't take him long to clock what first caught my eye. "Ninety minutes?"

"Like it was made for us." I take a deep breath. "And because I'm sometimes a chicken about the hard conversations, but maybe a clucking bird might be a way to diffuse some of the emotion around that."

"A chicken?" He frowns and looks from me to the bird, and back again. "It's a partridge."

"What? No, it's a chicken. It clucks."

"Partridges are in the chicken family."

I wrinkle my nose and look at the timer in his hand. In the context of it being sold at a Christmas market, it *might* be a partridge. "That makes it more random."

"No, it makes it perfect. Because you aren't a chicken." He twists the timer and sets the bird on the coffee table, where it starts clucking away quietly. Then he catches me by the waist and pulls me on top of him. "And maybe we need a bit of Christmas magic."

I straddle his hips. He curves one hand around my waist and trails the other up my body before curving his fingers around the back of my neck.

"You're beautiful," he murmurs.

I blush. "This isn't what I thought we'd do with the chicken."

"But maybe it's what we should do with the partridge." He pulls me in and groans at the first press of his lips to the corner of my mouth. "Missed this. Missed you."

I kiss him back, both of us breathing harder right away. His lips feel so good, so hungry and warm and firm as he works his way into my mouth.

His tongue strokes over mine in a possessive, claiming lick that makes me shiver.

And I should be all in on the kiss, I *am*, but—

"What is it?" He nuzzles my neck.

See? Observant.

"The clucking is distracting," I admit.

"I like it."

"Nothing fazes you."

He grazes the tendon on the side of my neck with his teeth. "I was fazed as fuck when I thought that doctor was flirting with you."

I suck in a breath. "He wasn't."

"My lizard brain didn't know that."

"I like him, though."

Garrett growls and rears up, flipping me onto my back, caging me beneath him.

I laugh and press my hands to his chest. "As a colleague."

"Colleague?" He notches his head to the side. "Are you thinking of moving back home?"

"No." I say it as quickly as I said it to Dr. Schmidt, but my pulse starts racing anyway.

"Then what do you mean?" He climbs off me, suddenly all serious.

The partridge chicken clucks ominously. We're five minutes into a ninety minute window and we're already done kissing.

"Don't pull away," he says, his voice low and steady, his gaze unwavering. "Stay in this moment with me."

I try to take a deep breath and it hurts.

"Hey, hey..." He comes back, taking my hands in his. "Be brave. You can tell me anything, Roar."

I shake my head. Just because he's willing to hear anything doesn't mean I can say it out loud.

He exhales, frustrated, but he doesn't let go of my hands.

I sag, my eyes dropping to the chicken clucking away on the coffee table. I can feel him following my gaze.

Cluck cluck cluck.

"Maybe you are chicken, after all," he finally says.

My head jerks up. "What?"

He shrugs. "I thought you were braver than this."

"Garrett!"

"Prove me wrong, then," he says with silky menace. "Be brave enough to tell me the scary thoughts inside your head."

"What are you doing?"

"Playing emotional chicken with my favourite person."

I let out a watery laugh. "You're joking."

"You're so strong, Rory. I can't cajole you into being soft for me. You like to fight. So let's face off. Come on. We've got..." He glances at the timer. "Eighty minutes left. Let's put it all on the table. You hate how calm I am."

I gasp. "No."

"It irritates you."

"That's not the same thing as *hate*. I actually love how calm you are, even when it prickles me."

His eyes light up, emerald flecks ablaze with hope so bright it takes my breath away. "Tell me more."

"Shut up. You tell me something now." I glare at him. "Emotional chicken goes both ways. Are you brave enough?"

"All right." He lets go of my hands, but he doesn't move away. He relaxes into the couch and stretches his arm over the back, curving around me without touching me. "I was wrong to say that you hate your job."

My insides flip flop.

He watches me closely, scrutinizing me, but his own expression is hard to read.

"This makes me mad," I admit. "Not knowing what you're thinking."

"I just told you."

"No, you told me that you thought you were wrong. You didn't say that you've changed your opinion."

"Can't get anything past you." He sighs. "I don't know what to think."

"Garrett! You said it was *unbearable* that I wasn't happy. Well, it's unbearable that you fixate on my job being the problem between us."

His eyes narrow. Not angrily. Probably thoughtfully, but I'm simmering now, so I read more into his expression.

It's so hard to stay present in the conversation. I want to jump up and run away, but the stupid clucking keeps me on the couch.

I'm not going to let him win this game of emotional chicken-partridge-truth wars.

"You're *so* mad about this," he finally murmurs. "Do you ever think about *why* you're so mad?"

"Why don't you tell me," I say sarcastically.

"Because it's not fucking fair. You fought so hard to get to where you are now, and you put so many years into this and so much money." He sighs. "For a long time, I just told myself that I can't be the person to tell you that you don't like your job, because I knew you didn't want to hear it. But now that I've said it out loud, I know it's not quite that simple. Because you love it, too. And it's so fucking complicated, isn't it? That's what makes you mad. I'm trying to reduce something complicated to a simple yes or no question."

Stunned, I just stare at him.

Four and a half years of queasy uncertainty.

"Is that close to the truth?" he asks softly.

"I hate my job," I whisper incredulously.

"But you don't hate being a doctor."

I shrug, helpless. "I don't know."

"Sometimes, it lights you up like nothing else."

I think about the ways his eyes can burn like fire when he looks at me. Do I sometimes feel that way about medicine? *Yes.* Without hesitation. But the endlessly complicated negotiations of working with a dozen conflicting personalities has drained me. And the people management part of being chief resident has destroyed me. And the way I had to throw myself into my residency, all or nothing, ruined my relationship. "Oh, my God, Garrett, what am I gonna do?"

"I don't know. Probably get mad some more."

I make a helpless sound that's part laugh, part sob. "That actually *is* unbearable."

He slides his fingers into my hair, gentle as can be. "No, mad I can handle. Mad is at least acknowledging that there's a problem here, even if we don't want to name what it is. The unhappy is...there's no fix for that. But mad, there are fixes for that."

"Like what?"

"I don't know that part yet. We— we're gonna sort that out."

We.

"I like the sound of we," I admit.

"Me, too." He takes a breath, then lets it out in a rush, and it's like a dam bursts. "I want you back. I regret leaving so much. I knew that I made a mistake immediately."

Both of us react to that. He snaps his spine straight, sitting up taller. Maybe he's surprised that he said that out loud, but I'm so glad he did, because I lean in and touch his arm, all the fight leaving me.

I don't want to play games.

I don't want to fight.

I want to know where we went wrong, and why we couldn't fix it last spring.

"It's okay," I whisper. "Tell me more."

He gives me a look like he's not sure he believes me.

And frankly, I don't blame him.

But when I don't look away, he starts talking again.

"Moving out was one of the hardest things I've ever done," he admits, his voice rough. "It felt like I was tearing myself in two, leaving the most important part of myself behind and stumbling out into the world as half a man.

"But I also knew that my happiness couldn't hinge on your happiness or on you, period. I needed to find something in myself, for myself, of myself. For the first time ever in my adult life, I got to ask myself the question, what do I want?" He stares at me now, really intently. More intently than he's ever looked at me before. "And at no point. *At no point*, were you not that answer."

I can't breathe.

He drags his hand to my shoulder, anchoring himself to me. "I've always wanted you. I will always want you."

"But...?"

The look on his face is so fragile.

I push up on my knees and wrap my arms around him. So he doesn't have to look at me, but he can hold me as he continues.

He presses his face into my neck, his words muffled now. "But when we were young, I thought that I needed you. You were my entire life, and when your life got really hard, it dragged me down in a way I couldn't make sense of. I was nothing but a support person, and you didn't want to be supported."

That's so hard to hear. So hard not to react to.

But I need to hear it, so I just keep holding him.

He kisses my neck, my jaw, and then presses his cheek to mine and exhales. "You know, when we were driving here, I was thinking about how excited you are to come home, that this is your home, and I don't have a home. Not like that. *You* were always my home.

"So this summer, for most of this year, I had to really get comfortable with the idea that I was a man without a home, and that I that I had to find a way to be okay, truly on my own, truly in myself."

"Garrett..."

"Let me get this out. I need to say more, Roar. Because I am okay without you, but I'm not great. I'm not fucking great, that's for sure.

"But it scares me too, because I can feel how easy it would be to sink back into you being my entire world, living and breathing for you. I like taking care of you, but I'm not sure that you like me taking care of you. I think it makes you feel helpless, maybe, and you're not. You're anything but. You're amazing. Because of you, babies are born safely and mothers survive when nature doesn't work out exactly as they wanted it to."

He eases back just enough to take my face in his hands. "I hear those stories from you, and I think you're fucking incredible."

"Thank you," I whisper.

Then I take a deep breath. "This isn't my only home. You asked me if I'm thinking of coming back here to work. The reason I said no is because I wouldn't make that decision without you. I'm not sure I'm cut out for a hospital position in Ottawa, either, but I haven't made a decision about where to go because I can't. It's felt like I've been stuck between a rock and a hard place, knowing I needed to leave, and not being able to leave where we built a life. In a way, you're my home, too. But I know what you're saying about that being problematic. I know I need to find my own happiness inside myself, and that's easier said than done."

"You'll find it," he promises. "And no matter what, you and me are forever some kind of *we*. You're my best friend."

"If I'm your best friend," I whisper, teasing, "why didn't you consult me before you pierced your fucking penis?"

He laughs. "Would you have told me not to?"

"No. I'd have gone with you and held your hand." I bite my lip for a moment, but since he's already admitted to jealousy... "I thought you got it because you met someone new and more exciting than me."

He groans and shakes his head. Staring at my mouth, he runs his thumb over my lip, where I'd just pressed my teeth. "There was nobody else. I got them for me, because I knew I'd be alone with my right hand for a long, long time. Maybe forever. I couldn't imagine moving on from you."

"Because I'm your best friend," I whisper against his thumb.

His gaze darkens, turns amber in the twinkling Christmas lights as my teeth graze his skin on *friend*.

"I want you to be more than that," he rumbles. "That's just the *no matter what* foundation."

"I've missed kissing you."

He moves in close. Not quite kissing, but almost. We will.

"And I've missed sleeping next to you. I love how warm you are."

He nods silently.

My heart is galloping now. "I've missed telling you that I love you."

"Tell me now."

"I love you so much. And it hurt so much to be apart."

"I'm sorry," he whispers against my mouth, his voice low and rough. Raw. "I'm sorry I hurt you. I've missed everything about you. I love you, too."

He kisses me, finally. Perfectly. Deeply.

"I love you with all that I am," he says on a rushed

breath between kisses as he pulls me back to straddle him again, this time with his back against the couch. "Can you be a quiet girl for me?"

"You might need to kiss me to shut me up."

"Don't have to tell me twice."

Chapter 29

Garrett

Rory is mine again, and the feel of her in my arms, the way she should be, is dizzying. No holding back, no denying where this intensity between us comes from.

Holding her tight against me, I roll us off the sofa and stretch her out on the floor. I'm obsessed with the way she stares up at me, soft wonder in her eyes.

"Kiss me," she whispers, and it's so soft and vulnerable and strong at the same time.

How did I ever let this woman go?

I couldn't keep my eyes off her all night. I kept staring at her mouth, her throat. Wanting to be the wine that she sipped and the happy gasp of air she'd pull in after a good laugh.

Now her mouth is mine, and I don't waste a second. I plunge into her, tasting her need. I swallow her moans until we're both out of breath, and then I cover her mouth with my hand as I kiss the rest of her.

Her neck.

The ridge of her ear, the soft biteable lobe.

Her breasts, as soon as I get her shirt rucked up. Her belly, her soft, quivering perfect softness.

I peel her long johns off and kiss lower still, my hand still covering her lips, feeling her pant against my fingers as I stretch my body taut, hitching her thighs over my shoulders.

There's no limit to how much I want her.

Her legs fall open as I nose my way closer and closer to the centre of her. She's so fucking pretty like this, all flushed and swollen and ripe for my tongue.

"I love you," I whisper right against her pussy, and she laughs against my hand, then tugs at my wrist.

"I'll be quiet," she promises.

Fuck it. I don't care if anyone hears us. After they all had a look at the dildo, they know what I'm about. They won't come downstairs.

I have eight long months to make up for.

This is how I should have been kissing her good night all fucking year.

Her breathing ticks up as I lick around her clit, her thighs flexing on either side of my head. I slide my fingers through her folds, needing to be inside her already.

And she needs that, too. "Please, Garrett."

"Yeah?" I tease her entrance.

"More."

I nip her inner thigh. "More? Greedy girl, you haven't even taken my fingers yet."

She rocks her hips, catching the tip of my two fingers, pulling me into her.

I groan-laugh. "That wasn't a challenge, you minx."

"Can't help it, I need you."

The breathy confession makes my cock flex against the floor, and the agonizing pleasure only intensifies as she squeezes down on my hand, surrounding my fingers with her tight, hot slickness.

"More," she begs.

I pump my fingers in and out of her, licking and sucking at her clit until her pleas reach a fevered pitch. Then I surge back up her body, still petting her eager cunt, pulling her slippery arousal out and coating her pussy with it as I plant my other arm on the floor beside her.

We stare at each other, breath mingling, gazes locked. I kiss her mouth again, suck on her tongue. None of it is enough. But it's all fucking perfect.

Her legs hitch up around my waist, grinding against me, pulling me down as we make out. My cock aches to be freed, to replace my fingers inside her.

I can't stop touching her, though.

"Get my cock out," I whisper.

She pushes my shirt off, first, then scrabbles for my waistband, shoving my pants down to my hips.

Her fingers on my throbbing flesh are the best thing I've ever felt.

I press my forehead against hers and hold her gaze. The whole room spins around us as I narrow in on Rory. "I want to be inside you bare. Have you been taking your pills?"

She nods.

"There hasn't been anyone else. There will never be anyone else but you."

"Make love to me, Garrett. Please. Don't hold back." Her eyes glitter up at me, a kaleidoscope of Christmas lights and unvarnished need. "I want everything you felt like you couldn't give me when we were apart."

She brings us together. My cock slips against her arousal, sliding heavy between her pussy lips.

Her head rolls back as my piercings bump over her clit.

"Fuck," I whisper.

"I know," she pants.

Reaching between us, I wrap my hand around hers, both of us working my cock against her now. Tangled and messy. It feels so good to rub on her, to hear her tiny sounds of pleasure, her hitching breath and ragged exhales every time we push my cock lower and tease her entrance.

"Take me," she pants. "Fuck me. I've missed you so much."

I can't hold back now. Not when she's saying stuff like that, making my heart beat so hard it feels like it's outside my body, trying to get to her. Into her. I cover her with my whole body, giving her my weight first, my hips between her lush thighs. And then, inch by inch, I work my cock into her body, watching her face the whole time.

"It's so good." Her eyelids flutter and she sucks in a breath as I get thicker, as I push deeper. Inexorably returning to her, returning to *us*.

Rolling my strokes, I look down between us, where she's stretched pink and perfect around me. "You feel so fucking tight, Roar. Like you're never going to let me go."

"I won't. I can't." Her voice breaks. "I love you so much."

I'll never take those words for granted ever again.

Groaning, I ease back, until my whole cock is glistening with her, and only the tip is hidden in her sweet body.

Her body quivers, her cunt clutching at the head of my shaft.

"Tell me you want more," I growl under my breath, for ears only. "Beg for my cock in your sweet pussy."

"More, yes, please. Give it to me."

I slam home, control slipping.

She clutches at my shoulders, silently gasping as I surge

all the way into her body. Lengthening my strokes, going balls deep every time. We find a rhythm that makes her shake, makes her wrap herself around me and cling for dear life. Every single inch of her rippling around me. She's going to milk me deep into her body before we're done here. But not before she comes. That will be what does it, feeling her come apart for me.

I yank her hips up, changing the angle, then plant one hand on the ground and find her clit with my other fingertips.

My Rory. Mine. My girl, forever and ever. My orgasms to give her. Mine.

She pumps her hips, fucking up at me now, both of us sweat slicked and feverish and needy and raw and real.

Her clit thickens and thrusts against my fingertips, then she's coming, and it's pulsing, and I feel it on my fingertips and around my cock at the same time, and it's everything.

"You're everything," I tell her as I let loose and thunder deep, burying myself inside her, following her into a release that's pure, unadulterated pleasure. She wraps herself around me, holding me tight as my cock pulses through the aftershock, until I come back into my head and find myself lying heavily on the love of my life.

"Sorry," I mumble as I give a half-hearted effort to detangle us.

"Stay," she whispers, and I give in to holding her like this, a messy twist of leaden limbs, heaving chests, and wildly beating hearts.

I kiss her damp chest as I ease out of her, then her belly, and then I nuzzle my way between her thighs.

"Can you come again?" I ask as I lick the mess we made together.

"I don't need to," she says, her breath hitching.

"That wasn't my question."

She stares down at me and nods. "Yes. Yes, please."

Carefully, because she's sensitive, I latch on to her clit, and I pull another orgasm from her tired, hardworking body. She trembles through this release like the very quiet girl she promised to be. I don't know how quiet we were in the middle there together, but this one, this one is definitely very quiet, and utterly beautiful.

When she finishes trembling on my face, I grab my t-shirt and use that to clean her up, what's left that I didn't devour.

And then I wrap myself around her instead of dressing her immediately, because it feels like if I let go of her for even a second, I might come apart at the seams.

It's Rory who finally flutters back to earth, who finds her long johns and disappears briefly to go pee, and then returns and finds me a clean shirt. Probably tucks away the evidence of our secret, reckless, wild floor fuck, too.

Turns the partridge timer off, the quiet clucking ending with a panicked little squawk at the end that sounds suspiciously like a chicken.

Then she tugs me up to the couch, and we tumble under a blanket together, her curled up in front of me, and fall into the best sleep either of us have probably had in almost a year.

Chapter 30

Rory

It's still dark when my alarm goes off. Garrett is a big, warm, heavy blanket all around me. One of his hands is under my shirt, cupped around my ribs but his thumb is hooked around the side of my boob, and his other arm is under me, possessively cupping my belly.

His thick erection is saying good morning, too, even if the rest of him is still mostly asleep.

"I'm going to grab a super quick shower," I whisper.

He doesn't move.

But when I tiptoe back downstairs, he's in the kitchen making coffee.

"Morning," he says gruffly, his voice still full of sleep.

Then he pulls me tight against me and kisses my damp hair, my forehead, my nose, and then finally my lips.

"Good morning," I whisper against his kiss. "You don't need to drive me. I can—"

"I want to. You might want to talk in the truck." He grins. "And besides. The less time your mom has to spend looking me in the eye this trip, the better for all of us."

"She was great last night."

231

"She was." He chuckles. "And me getting out of her hair today is a reward for that."

At the hospital, we visit Dani first, who is discouraged to report that she's still bleeding, but when I check her chart, I see that it's greatly reduced overnight.

"Did you get to hear the heartbeat this morning?" I ask.

She immediately brightens up. "Yes. Nice and strong."

"That's what we like to hear."

Jake arrives a few minutes later. He looks like he slept in a pile of kids, and Garrett immediately offers to go in search of coffee for him, even though we had big Thermoses on the drive down from Pine Harbour.

I leave Jake and Dani to have some time alone, and go to find Dr. Schmidt. The breech baby from the night before had converted to a c-section in the middle of the night after attempting a vaginal delivery, so he never ended up leaving.

"I got a few hours sleep in between, though. It's turning into an eventful two days here. And tomorrow is our weekly clinic day when we see every pregnant person in Bruce and Grey County." He grins. "A slight exaggeration. The midwifery clients don't come in unless there's a complication. You can come if you're a glutton for work."

"We're driving back to Ottawa tomorrow, otherwise you know I would. All the OBs have clinic on the same day?"

"Yep. There's only four of us right now. It's jammed but manageable."

"How many deliveries do you do each year?"

He starts rhyming off numbers. How many births the

whole hospital sees—seven hundred a year, which surprises me for how quiet the ward has been yesterday and today—how the docs split up the calendar, how many midwives have admitting privileges. And then he shrugs. "You'd have to ask my assistant. I can remember all of the faces of the delivering moms, but numbers? I'm not a numbers guy. How about you?"

I can't imagine just going with the flow like that. "Two hundred and three this year. Not all actively involved in, but c-sections scrubbed in for, or births assisted with."

He rocks back on his heels. "That's a lot."

"Yeah. But that's the life, right?"

He shrugs. "Yeah. Most places."

That shrug sticks with me as a nurse swings by to tell us the procedure room is ready for us. There's another resident with us this morning, a friendly family medicine PGY2. As he's scrubbing up, Schmidt pulls me aside.

"Would you mind doing some teaching with Dr. Kumar this morning? Dani has already said she's fine with having an extra observer."

"Of course. I just assumed."

"You're a guest here. I wouldn't impose if you weren't willing."

That sticks with me, too.

So the procedure takes a little longer than usual, but it's good.

And when I walk back to Dani's room with her on her stretcher, a kernel of an idea starts to bloom.

Schmidt joins us a few minutes later with discharge papers.

"Take it easy. Let your husband do everything."

"On it," Jake says, dead seriously.

"You might have cramping and more bleeding over the

next couple of days, but that's normal. I texted Kerry and she said she has a handheld doppler you can borrow to keep hearing the heartbeat."

"I ordered one online last night," Dani confesses.

"Try to use it sporadically. Don't let it become your arbiter of the pregnancy progression, all right? But I think you'll be fine. And I'll see you in my clinic in two weeks."

"Thank you."

Garrett holds out my coat. "Ready to go to cousin lunch?"

"Yep." I blow kisses to Dani and Jake. "You'll be missed today."

"Tell them all she's resting," Jake says, worry pinching at the corners of his eyes.

"I don't think he's going to let her lift a finger for the next six months," Garrett says as we head down the corridor.

I agree. "That bed rest might stretch into the post-partum period, and frankly, that sounds delighful."

Garrett looks at me sideways. "Yeah? So if we ever..."

"Bite your tongue. I mean, yes, we can have kids. But you can't pull that bossy shit with me."

He laughs. "Two things can be true, babe. You're the bossy one in our relationship, and I'll still be laying down the rest law if anything ever happens to you in pregnancy. And now I know who to call if I need another doc to lecture you." He jerks his thumb back in the direction of where Schmidt is working. "That guy."

"Wow, you went from jealous to conspiring with the guy in less than twenty-four hours!"

He tugs me close. "I'm confident that you're all mine. No need to be jealous when I can still feel you clenching around me."

I bury my face in his chest, blushing like mad.

But I'm smiling so hard my cheeks hurt, too.

The sun is shining for the drive back to Pine Harbour. The snow that fell last night glitters like crystals in all directions, a totally different vibe from when we first arrived, but the roads are clear.

"How attached are you to Ottawa?" I finally blurt out. "Like this rugby team you joined...what sort of a commitment did you make?"

"Is that what you've been churning about over there?" He shifts his hand on the steering wheel so he can reach across the console and squeeze the back of my neck. "It's a rec league thing. I'm sure I can find a team anywhere else. Why, are you thinking of moving to Australia or the UK?"

"I was thinking a little closer to home. Not forever. I know you don't love it here, but the pace of work would be better for me. I don't even know if they'd want me, not really, but I'm pretty good at horning my way into things, and if worst came to worst, I could pick up shifts at a walk-in clinic or sign up for a family medicine re-training, or—"

"Whoa, okay, slow down. You've jumped way past where I was thinking you were going."

I scrub my hands over my face. "I don't want to be a big city hospitalist."

"That's great."

"Well, it's...something. Those are like, ninety percent of the jobs. And I have a mountain of student debt."

"I'm pretty sure even small town family docs make enough to eventually pay that back."

"I don't know if I want to manage a practice of my own, though, either. And I know how that sounds."

"How do you think that sounds?"

"Like I'm spoiled and I don't want to do the hard work of being a grown up."

"You want to lean into your strengths and not get weighed down by stuff that stresses you out," he gently corrects. "Plus, you miss the tree farm. Honestly, I was fully expecting you to say you wanted to quit medicine and take over from your parents so they could retire."

I gape at him. "What?"

He shrugs. "I'd have gone along with that, too."

"No."

"Yes." He nods for good measure. "If you would be genuinely happy doing that, I'd be in, one hundred percent. I can fix cars and be in the army just about anywhere in the country. And if you wanted to go to Australia, I'd give it all up to be a rugby-playing house husband."

"I don't want to take over the tree farm. All of my fears about running my own practice would be tenfold worse trying to run my own farm." I take a deep breath. "Oh. That's probably where my fear comes from, isn't it?"

"Probably. I read somewhere that deep down, we're just our younger selves, constantly trying to process the world around us through the lens of what was going on around us when we were forming our permanent memories. Like, eight, nine, ten, eleven, twelve years old."

"You read that? I'm impressed."

He laughs out loud. "Okay, I saw it on the internet. I watched a lot of self-help content while we were broken up."

"Still sounded good."

"Some of those apps are wild. It was like it knew that I was a miserable fuck who missed his girlfriend and wanted to figure out what went wrong."

"I don't want you to be miserable again, if we move."

He rubs his thumb along the back of my neck. "I'll tell you if I am. And we'll tackle it together."

"We can't live at the farm, though."

"God no. Cassie only lasted a day and a half. You wouldn't make it six hours." He shrugs. "We can rent a place to start? See how we like it. And if we don't, then we'll move somewhere else."

"Just like that?"

He exhales and shakes his head. "Not just like that, babe. That took a year of being miserable, eight months of being broken up, a dozen ninety minute fights, you ovulating just extra enough to break down and need me, and a dead car battery to get to this point."

"Well, when you put it like that..."

He slows down at the turn to Pine Harbour. "Yeah. I think this was a hard won gentle victory."

I reach over and stroke the back of his neck as he needs both hands to make the turn.

And then as soon as he parks at Mac's Diner, he tangles our fingers together and tugs me across the console for a kiss.

"I want you to be happy, too," I whisper against his mouth. "I want to find a place where we *both* want to be."

"Shut up and kiss me."

I'm laughing against his lips when there's a knock at the truck window.

"You really want to move back to this town?" Garrett is grumbling. "Can't even kiss my girl in peace."

But as soon as he twists around, his expression changes to one of pure joy.

"Hey, buddy," he says after lowering his window.

A big cowboy leans in and smiles at me. "You must be Rory. I heard all about you yesterday. I'm Zane."

"Yeah, same." I shake his hand. "You want to go inside?"

"For sure. You guys want to finish your kissing first? I'll give you some privacy." He winks and thumps Garrett on the shoulder.

"We're good." I scramble out of the truck.

Garrett catches me at the front, and in front of his new cousin and everyone else in the lot, he sweeps me into a big, hungry, dipping kiss.

"I'll say when we're good," he growls against my lips.

I roll my eyes, but my cheeks are hot with pleasure at the possessive claim.

Then it's time to initiate Zane in Boxing Day cousins lunch at Mac's.

Garrett doesn't let me go until we're inside, and we're sliding into one of four reserved booths.

Zane slides in across the way, with their cousin Owen, who drove him to the diner. Jules and Cassie arrive next, and then it's an endless parade of Minellis and Kincaids, until every booth is full.

"Where's Kerry?" I quietly ask Owen as I slide out from the booth, making room for his youngest brother, Adam.

"She's checking on Dani," he says. "She might come a bit later, but she also has some paperwork to catch up on at the clinic, so she's taking advantage of Becca being home to have a childfree afternoon."

"It's Boxing Day!"

He shrugs, grinning shamelessly. "She loves her job,

loves her clinic. Getting everything neatly in order is her happy place."

Garrett catches my eye and I smile at him. Then the conversation pivots to army stuff. Like Garrett and his cousins, Zane was in the army, one of many similarities the cousins have discovered over the last two days, although he got out when they bought their mom a ranch in southern Alberta.

Owen nods at Garrett. "How's training going in 33 CBG?"

"Good. You know." He glances my way again. "Won't be there much longer. Roar's almost finished her training, and we're not sure where we're going next."

"Would you guys ever move back in this direction?"

Garrett's still looking at me, his gaze hot and searching.

I nod slightly.

"Yeah, we might just. I'll keep you posted."

"We'd love to have you in the regiment."

I lose the rest of the army conversation there, jargon and half-sentences that only they understand. But I like the look on Garrett's face.

He's always had complicated feelings about Pine Harbour, but maybe coming home might be good for him. And if it's not, we won't stay. I know that with my whole heart now.

I float over to the table where Rafe and Olivia are sitting with my Jules and Cassie. Our cousins Tom and Zander are right behind them. We catch up, and then their food arrives.

I catch the waitress before she heads back to the kitchen. "Can my lunch be put in a takeaway container?"

"Sure."

I head back to our table. "Owen, do you think Kerry would mind a drop in at the clinic?"

He shakes his head. "For you? Anything."

I gesture for Garrett to stay sitting. "I'm going to walk down there. Come pick me up when you're done. No rush."

I collect my lunch at the counter, then put on my coat and head out into the brisk sunshine before my sisters can catch my eye. It's a gorgeous day for a walk through town, but I want to take it by myself.

Kerry's midwifery clinic is right in the heart of town, where two days ago the street was shut down for the Christmas market.

Today, it's super quiet. All the stores are closed for Boxing Day, but there is a light on at the clinic, and when I try the door, it's open.

"Hello?" I call out.

"Back here!" Kerry's head pops out from the office. "Hey! What are you doing here?"

"I left Garrett at Cousin Lunch and brought my French fries to share with you." I hold up the takeout bag. "I have some questions, and I think you're the right woman to answer them."

It's not Garrett who picks me up. Jules and Cassie barrel into the clinic an hour later.

"You snuck out," Jules protests. "And I need to leave ASAP."

"Although when you find out where Jules is going, you won't feel bad about ditching her," Cassie adds. "But it's true that we don't get much time with you."

I glance at Kerry.

She beams back.

"Well," I say slowly, drawing out the word. "By the end of the summer, Cassie will be able to find me here at least once a week. And then it'll be *your* problem that we don't see you often enough, Baby!"

Jules gasps. "You're moving home?"

I nod. "For a trial year. To see if we like it, and if there's enough work for an OB to have a clinic day here once a week. I'm burned out."

It's a relief to say it out loud.

And then I burst into tears.

"Oh, Mini," Jules whispers, shoving Cassie at me.

They wrap around me, and from a distance, Kerry asks if anyone wants tea.

"Mom is going to be so worried about your student loans," Jules whispers.

"Shut up, Baby," Cassie whispers back. "Mini will figure it out. She always does."

"Still, maybe don't tell Mom for a while."

I wince. "That does sound like a classic Rory coping strategy, but no, I think it'll be fine."

Cassie nods. "Garrett won't let them bully you."

I take a deep breath. "Speaking of Garrett... We broke up in April."

"What?" my sisters say in unison.

Jules wrinkles her nose. "Then why were there kissing noises coming from the back room last night?"

I make a choking sound.

She winks. "Just kidding, I didn't hear anything, but now I know you guys were smooching. So what happened? When did you get back together?"

I glance at Cassie.

She shrugs. "It's okay. No Bechdel Test today."

"Like...maybe in August? And then maybe in September. Not in October or November, as much as I wanted to, but then last week. And last night kind of cemented us back together."

"I'm confused." Jules laughs. "But I don't care! A second chance love story for Mini! Maybe there's hope yet for Middle."

"Bite your tongue." Cassie glowers. "The last person I'm having any kind of love story with is my husband."

Kerry brings us a tea tray, and we fill my sisters in on the business plan we're going to propose to the OBs at the hospital. There are enough high-risk patients like Dani on the peninsula, who have to drive all the way into town for their clinic appointments, that I can take some of that pressure and see those patients a bit closer to home, and integrate their care more closely with Kerry and her partner Jenna. We can test it for a year, and then take stock on how it's working for everyone. Low risk, fascinating data, and a break from the hospitalist life for me.

"To Rory's next adventure," Jules says.

"And to having one of my sisters back home with me for my return to single hood," Cassie adds.

I clink their mugs. "Cheers. Now Jules, where are you going that you need to rush back to nannying?"

She screws up her face in an excited squeal. "We're going to the Bahamas."

"Oh for fuck's sake, get out of here," I say, laughing and waving her off. "How much do you get paid to be nanny to the stars, again?"

"More than you." She sticks out her tongue.

"Bitch," I say warmly. But I'm proud of her. Nothing seems impossible for our fearless little sister.

When we step out into the sunshine, Jules' car isn't the only vehicle in front of the clinic.

Garrett is leaning against his truck, a slow smile on his face.

"See you at the farm, lovebirds," Cassie says, pushing me towards him.

"I told them," I say as he pulls me into his arms.

"And?"

"And they're happy for us."

"Good. Me, too."

I laugh.

"Come on, I want to show you something Will mentioned to me before we head to the farm."

He helps me into the passenger seat, then jogs around the truck.

We don't go far. He drives over to the community school, a K-12 sprawling building.

"This brings back memories," I tease. "Parking at the school on a day it's closed. You looking to get lucky?"

"I think your mom wants us back faster than that."

I blow a raspberry. "She can wait."

He winks. "I think your aunt and uncle have left, so we can have your bed to ourselves tonight. I can be patient. Anyway, I wanted to show you..." He leans over and takes my hand, pointing to the school sign, and the mascot below it, which hasn't changed since we were students here.

THE PINE HARBOUR PANTHERS

243

Under the sign, though, are a few more sports teams than I remember. And right at the end: *Rugby*.

"I think I've found my new rugby team," he murmurs. "Coaching might be a fun challenge next year."

I turn my head just enough to see his face. To see that he's smiling, and it's soft and happy and real. "Yeah?"

"Yep."

"Good." A warm, delicious feeling—happiness in its purest form—bubbles up inside me and comes out on a soft laugh. "Because I think I've already hung my shingle on Main Street."

Epilogue

---

six months later

Garrett

"No, that box is for the bedroom."

I suppress a smile as Rory grabs the little plastic zip container that holds her allergy eye drops, lip balm, and snail mucus under eye patches, all from her *bedside table*, and shoves that into a box marked *Bathroom*.

Packing brings out her bossiest tendencies. It's cute and exasperating at the same time.

"Those live on your bedside table."

"But they're toiletries. They only live on a bedside table in a completely put together bedroom. They shouldn't be unpacked in the bedroom." Sure in her logic, she adds two more bundles of things from the bathroom on top, and then seals up the box. "Okay, that's good to go."

"When your eyes are scratchy and we haven't unpacked the bathroom stuff yet—"

"I have a spare set of drops in my backpack."

I'm about to argue further, because it's fun to rile her up, but her pager goes off.

Today is technically a day off, for us to pack up the last of our belongings before her final shifts at the hospital.

Wincing, she grabs the pager and reads the screen.

When we left Pine Harbour the day after Boxing Day, we spent the whole road trip back to Ottawa talking about our lives together, our future, and how we would survive the last six months of her residency training.

Because Rory becoming a fully-trained doctor is a goal worth making some sacrifices for, but we lost each other once and we didn't want to risk that again.

The partridge timer became an integral part of our "hang in there" plan.

Once a week, on a day Rory isn't on call, we give each other a guaranteed-uninterrupted ninety minutes. At first, we used it to talk. Some weeks we used it for sex. And then we started to use it for...doing things. Playing cards. Going for a walk.

And for six months, not a week has gone by that Rory hasn't made those timer dates a priority.

Until, maybe, today.

Because today is the day of the week we were going to do that—after we finished packing.

But last night, a twin mom who Rory has been following in and out of antenatal over the last six weeks went into labour.

"Go," I say, even before she has to explain what she's reading on the screen.

"I might only be an hour or two," she promises.

I know better.

And this time, it's all right. More than all right. "As much as I want to bicker about packing all day, I can handle this myself. Go. Be with your patient."

"We weren't bickering."

"As soon as you're gone, I'm opening up that box and putting the shit you keep on your bedside table in the *Bedroom* box."

Her mouth drops open, then snaps shut.

I take her chin in my hand and lift her face. "Do you want to get ice cream tonight?"

Her expression softens. "One last gelato in Little Italy before I drag you back to Pine Harbour?"

"Exactly." I rub my thumb against her bottom lip, enjoying the way she holds still for me, how her mouth drags open and her expression goes soft. "Roar, don't feel badly about going to the hospital today."

"I don't," she whispers, but her voice hitches.

She does.

And she wants to go anyway.

"There's never enough time, but we always make time. And we have."

"But we need to pack."

"I want you to imagine for a second that I'm capable of completing the packing job that I've already done ninety percent of."

Her eyes narrow. "I've helped as much as I can."

"Sure. Yes. I know."

"Garrett!"

"Go to work."

"We're going to argue about this later," she snaps.

I grin. "I'm counting on it."

"I'm sorry I'm late, I'm sorry—"

I catch Rory as she comes flying into the condo. She's still in scrub pants and a t-shirt that says *Show Me Your Uterus.* "It's okay."

She huffs out a breath and a curl that came loose from her double French braid bounces against her forehead. "Give me fifteen minutes to shower and change."

"No rush. The ninety minutes doesn't start until we're both ready."

She brushes a kiss against my mouth and then runs to the shower. The water cranks on, then off. When she sprints out of the bathroom barely wrapped in a towel, water droplets still clinging to her, I follow her to the bedroom.

Suddenly I'm less interested in ice cream and more interested in chasing those droplets with my tongue.

"Don't," she warns as she briskly dries herself off, making everything jiggle.

"Why not?" I waggle my eyebrows at her.

"We're running out of time to appreciate our neighbourhood."

I tip my head back and laugh. I don't bother pointing out that she walks through Little Italy every day, going to and from the hospital. What she's really saying is, we need to take one of our precious blocked-out date moments and focus on the good that we had here.

Something specific to remember and hold in our hearts.

So licking my way between her tits and down her belly will have to wait until after we get gelato.

Fine.

I lean against the doorway and cross my arms. "All right. But slow down, let me appreciate you getting dressed first."

She rolls her eyes, but then takes her time stretching her

arms high over her head, making her tits bounce, as she slides her arms into a t-shirt.

By the time she's zipping up her jeans, I'm half hard and completely dialled in.

"Ready to go?"

"Mmhmm." She picks up the partridge timer. "Never too late, right?"

"Never."

She turns it to the full hour and a half. "And...start."

Hand in hand, we stroll the few blocks to the gelato shop. Her fingers feel so good woven through mine. Strong little fingers. Sure little fingers. Hands that are so steady when she's doing surgery, and so soft when she's welcoming a baby into the world.

And personally, so very clever when she touches me.

I rub my thumb against her skin, and she looks up at me. "How are you feeling about being done at the garage?"

I shrug. I liked some of the guys I worked with, but people come and go. This week it was my turn to go. "I'm mostly excited to get the rest of the move done."

On my days off this month, I've been driving back and forth to Pine Harbour on my own. First it was to find us a rental house. Then I took a load of boxes to the farm. Then I got the keys to the house, and dropped off the couch Rory bought when we were broken up. The couch we hooked up on the first time and that I'll cherish forever.

That most recent trip, Rory's mom talked her way into getting a spare set of keys so she could clean our rental house top to bottom.

"Hey, remind me to get that key back from my mom," Rory says, reading my mind.

I chuckle. "I was just thinking that. If we aren't careful,

she's going to use that key to let herself in one day and hear something she won't want to hear."

Rory snickers. "Maybe that would be a good lesson for her to learn."

I give her a stricken look.

"No," she says solemnly. "Of course not."

"It's bad enough that she's held the eggplant version of my dick."

Rory giggles.

"Okay, let's focus. What kind of gelato do you want?"

"Pistachio," she says immediately. "You?"

"Chocolate."

She smiles happily.

After we get our treats, we move away from the noise of the street, heading down the side street until we find a bench.

"Do you want to try some of the pistachio?" Rory scoops a little of her gelato on her spoon and holds it out for me.

"Yep."

She tries my chocolate next, and then we sit quietly and finish our scoops. I finish faster than her, so I just watch her eat.

Around us, the city hums with a quiet vibrancy.

I'm going to miss this a bit. Not enough to think we'll move back, but even with the ups and downs, Ottawa has been really good to us.

After six gruelling—and yes, sometimes miserable—months finishing her residency, it feels like a gift to have this final moment together in the city where we became adults. Where I joined the army and became a mechanic. Where Rory charged through her degrees and training with breathtaking ease—from the outside—and became a doctor, and a surgeon.

And then, over the last six months, she bloomed into an even brighter, stronger version of herself.

She scrapes the last bit of gelato out of her paper cup, then tips her head to the side. "Why are you looking at me like that?"

"Have I told you that I really love who you've become?"

Her face softens even further, impossibly tender, as she smiles up at me. "Yes. But you can tell me again."

"I do. You are amazing."

Her eyes crinkle with delight. "I love you, too. And I'm excited for what comes next for us, you know? We're going to do that together."

"Absolutely." I slant my mouth against hers. "Forever together."

Rory

Two days later, we mount up for a final road trip to Pine Harbour.

Garrett drives his truck, with our bed frame in the back, the last thing to leave our condo. I drive my brand-new SUV, a graduation present from Garrett. It's a more rugged vehicle that's perfect for stuffing full of boxes for this move, and will be equally perfect for winters on the peninsula. Way better than the hatchback I bought last year. He fixed that up and we sold it this spring.

We stop twice for coffee, but otherwise it's just a hard press to get home.

When we arrive late in the afternoon, there's a welcome party.

"This is too many people," I say to Garrett under my breath.

Not quiet enough for my mother not to hear.

"Many hands make light work," she says pointedly. "Don't be afraid of help."

Mom still hasn't gotten over me not telling her about the breakup. Luckily, her being hurt and me being annoyed hasn't stopped either of us from being excited that we're finally home.

Now, I throw my arms around her neck and buss a kiss on her cheek. "I love your help, Mom."

Jules sails past with a box from the car.

"Is that the one marked *Christmas*?" I call out. "That can go in the spare room."

She shakes her head. "No, it's *Bedroom*!"

"Oh, excellent. I want to make the bed up first." Then I see Dani step out from inside the house, with her brand new baby in her arms. "But not before saying hello to the newest little Foster!"

"Do you want to hold her?" Dani asks.

"You don't have to ask me twice," I coo, taking her sweet, soft, fresh-smelling daughter in my arms. "Oh, how sweet are you?"

"You've had a long drive. Maybe a baby cuddle might be a good excuse to take a minute to yourself while you let the family unload?"

"I'm fine," I whisper, but I've already buried my nose against the top sweet newborn scalp.

Then, arms happily full, I follow Dani inside.

"I filled your fridge a bit," she says as she leads me into my own kitchen.

"You just had a baby!"

"I was on and off bedrest for six months. As soon as this little one arrived, I vaulted back to life. And I wanted to cook for my family, so I was just making extra." She leans back against the counter after making sure we're alone. "And now we can hide here while everyone else brings in boxes."

Many hands do make light work—my mother was right—and in less than an hour, all the boxes are in their designated rooms.

Jules tries to start unpacking, but Garrett stops her and corrals her into the kitchen.

"I'm just trying to help," she protests. "I came all the way to be useful!"

"But it's beer and pizza time now," I tell her. "Come and sit with Dani and me. Tell us about your fancy bosses. Where are they spending the summer?"

"He's staying in Toronto. She's filming on location, so I'm flying back and forth with the kidlet."

"First class?" I tease.

"Of course."

Dani and I look at each other.

"Of course," we repeat, both of us deadpan.

Jules rolls her eyes. "Can I go back to unpacking now?"

"Just sit with us," I tease, knowing it will rile her up more. "I'm kidding. Sure. If you want to be really helpful, you could set up my bed!"

Garrett's head lifts from the conversation he was having with his cousin.

"We already set up the bed frame," he says over the din of chatter. Then his gaze falls to the baby in my arms, and he gets this stupidly goofy smile on his face.

My tummy flutters.

Nearby, Jake has finished eating his slice of pizza.

"Hey, Dad, time for you to hold your daughter," I say, pretending like I don't want to snuggle her all night long.

But I should probably supervise my sister.

He takes the little one into the crook of his arm, and I dart for the stairs. There are three rooms up here, two of them big enough to be bedrooms, the last one more of an office—or a nursery. Right now, it's completely empty. But because of our breakup, we have two beds, so we're setting up our bedroom and a spare room.

The biggest bedroom also has a gorgeous big window that overlooks the quiet backyard, and I stop in the doorway, appreciating the lovely calm of it all. My mom must have been up here, too, because the bed is already made.

Jules is going through boxes efficiently, hanging stuff up in the closet. I open the last box and laugh when I see the little plastic bundle of my bedroom toiletries right on top.

I set it on my pillow, since we don't actually have the bedside tables up here yet, and carry the rest of the box over to where my sister is standing in front of the closet. "This stuff needs to be put on the shelves in here."

"I'll get out of your way and start next door," she says.

"Are you girls up here?" my mom calls out, climbing the stairs again.

"I'm in the bedroom," I say. "We're almost done in here."

"Spare room next, Mama," Jules says, twirling away from me.

I grin at her. "Isn't this fun? Don't you want to move home, too?"

"Some of us are meant to—"

An ear-shattering scream next door cuts Jules off.

We both race into the spare room just in time to see my

mother lob the eggplant dildo in the air. Jules catches it, then realizes what's in her hands, and wings it at me.

I clutch it to my chest.

"Aurora," my mother says reproachfully. "Why did you make me touch that thing again?"

Jules snickers under her breath.

"Shut up," I snap at her. "Mom, I didn't make you touch anything. That was in the *Christmas* box! You didn't need to open it!"

Jules schools her features into fake sincerity. "Why is your dildo in a box marked *Christmas*?"

"Don't use that word," my mother says.

"Christmas?" Jules and I say at the same time. And then, "Oh, *dildo*."

"Girls!"

"Relax, Mom," I say, because I've had six months to reconcile myself to the fact this is simply funny and not mortifyingly embarrassing. For me, anyway. "I'm planning on giving it back to Garrett this Christmas as a joke. We haven't, uh, used it."

"I should hope not." She shakes her head as I grab the Christmas box, tuck the dildo away, and put the whole thing in the closet. "That's doesn't look comfortable."

"You know it's modelled after—"

I cut Jules off. "She doesn't need that reminder, Baby."

"Nobody needed that reminder, Mini, but here we are!"

"Okay, time for you to go back to your jet-setting ways."

But Jules is on a melodramatic roll now, enjoying our mom's discomfort. "I shouldn't have to see, much less *hold*, my brother-in-law's eggplant facsimile more than once in my life!"

"Juliana Minelli, that's enough." My mom lets out a watery laugh. "But also, same."

I give her a rueful smile. "Hey, maybe let this be a warning that you shouldn't use your key uninvited."

She gasps, and then we're all laughing so hard our sides hurt.

The last box to get opened is a small one for the kitchen. It literally says *Kitchen: Last Box to Open* on it, and Garrett has it in his hands when the last of our excited guests leave. We wave goodbye from the porch, then he hands the box to me and ushers me back inside.

"Want to do the honours?"

I carry it back to the kitchen. A stack of flattened cardboard boxes is on the table, but it actually looks like a home already.

"I can't believe we're basically fully moved in," I say as I slice the tape open. "What's left?"

"The most important part." Garrett wraps his arms around me from behind, nuzzling my neck.

Inside the box is the partridge timer, sitting on top of Garrett's green flannel shirt.

"Oh, of course," I whisper. "It needs to go in a place of honour, doesn't it?"

"I was thinking..." He takes it from the box and moves around me, twisting it to start a ninety minute countdown before setting it on an open shelf. "Right in the heart of our home."

"Nice." I lean against the counter. "What do you want to talk about?"

His eyes crinkle. "Anything you want. How was your drive?"

I laugh. "Yeah, pretty good. Had a fun convoy partner. Yours?"

"Easy. Spent the whole time thinking about this."

"Unpacking?"

He grins. "The whole thing. Unpacking. Watching you snuggle a little baby, and then turn all pink when I caught you sniffing the top of her head. Hearing the inevitable Minelli shrieks of laughter."

"They found the dildo again."

That makes him groan. "Oh, God."

"Yeah. But on the upside, I don't think my mom will be letting herself into the house. I suggested she might find us using it right here on the counter."

His eyes light up.

"Not exactly," I hasten to add.

"But we should." He draws me close and kisses me hungrily. "We will."

I wrap my arms around his neck, eager for more. But then I remember. "Hey, you re-packed my eye drops and lip balm!"

"I told you I was going to." He kisses the corner of my mouth. "I think what you mean to say is, *you were right, Garrett.*"

"Doubtful," I mutter.

"I want to hear it." He's laughing.

"I had to put it on my pillow because the bedside tables weren't upstairs yet."

"The horror," he mocks.

And I can't pull away, because the partridge is clucking. So I tighten my arms around his neck and kiss his stupid right mouth until he stops laughing.

I love the way his whole body gets into kissing me. He curves over me, surrounding me with love so warm it feels like a cozy blanket, and he gathers me close.

He tastes like beer and pizza, and he feels like home.

When he turns me and picks me up, putting me on the little kitchen island, I think it's because he's going to wedge his big body between my legs and do some more kissing.

Instead, he breaks away, his chest heaving, and gestures to the box. "Now put on that shirt."

I blink at it. We both love this shirt, and we take turns claiming ownership over it.

"Okay." I'm laughing softly at him as I tug it out of the box, but my giggle dies as a velvet box tumbles out, too.

Garrett catches it with ease.

My hands go numb.

"The shirt, Roar," he nudges.

I nod, but I don't move.

He helps me, sliding my arms into the soft, familiar cotton. He adjusts the collar around my neck, then tugs the front, making sure it's all around me before he sinks to one knee.

I already can't breathe.

I'm perched on the kitchen island like a princess on a pedestal, and he's bowing before me like a knight in my court.

"Aurora Minelli, I have wanted to ask you this question since the first time you kissed me. But I was a skinny little teenager then, and you were the smartest girl in school. I didn't know that you'd let me tag along as you set off to pursue your dreams.

"But being a part of your life ever since has been the second greatest gift you've ever given me. Getting a chance to win you back is the only thing that nudges it out of top spot. I will follow you to the ends of the earth, but tonight, it feels like we've come full circle.

"So tonight feels like the right time to finally speak these words out loud, the words I've held in my heart since I was a boy." He takes a deep breath, and holds my blurry gaze.

I swipe at my cheeks and try to smile, but it's so hard because my lips are wobbling.

"Will you marry me? Will you be my wife? Will you let me be your husband in every way, on every day, for the rest of my life?"

"Yes," I whisper. And then louder, "Yes, yes, please."

He opens the ring box, and the prettiest diamond I've ever seen sparkles up at me.

Behind me, the partridge clucks in approval.

"Oh, Garrett."

He stands up, and *now* he wedges himself between my legs. He takes my hand and kisses my fingertips, my knuckles, before sliding the ring onto my finger.

"It's so beautiful," I whisper.

"You're beautiful," he murmurs back.

"This is a dream." I kiss him.

"My dream," he says in between that kiss and the next. And the next after that is so deep, so long, that we're still kissing when the timer goes off.

Breathless, we both turn and look at it.

He takes a firm grip of his flannel shirt, wrapped around me, and says, "Stay right here, my wife-to-be."

"Staying," I manage to breathe.

He looks huge as he grabs the timer. All of his muscles are flexed, his whole body tense. He's gorgeous. And mine, all mine, again. For always this time. Forever.

Instead of just stopping the timer, he cranks it around, all the way. "That was a pretty good start," he says, setting it back on the shelf. "Let's see what we can do with another ninety minutes."

Rory and Garrett do eventually use the eggplant facsimile! To get a spicy Christmas do-over short story, straight to your inbox, where Garrett tells Rory how pretty she is riding his silicon copy, visit www.zoeyork.com/the-christmas-do-over!

Plus www.zoeyork.com/bonus-content has *all* the extras, including character art and Rory's Christmas music playlist.

If you are new to Pine Harbour and want to keep reading, Rafe and Olivia Minelli's second chance romance is available in Love in a Small Town.

Acknowledgements

The dedication for this book comes from a comment in The Smuthood Facebook group by Nicolette L. that made me bust a gut ... because it's so true, a lot of my books are slow burn for the spice, and this one is decidedly not.

I owe so much to Brighton, Annika, Selena, and Molly, who workshopped many of these scenes with me as I developed this story over a year and a half.

Brighton also helped me connect with Newton Henrique, who did custom character art for Rory and Garrett (check out the bonus content section of my website if you want to see more of that!). And the whole "it takes a village" continues, because another author, Lena, helped me find the photo for the ebook cover, a Wander Aguiar image.

I'm always so grateful for romancelandia.

When it came time for copyedits, I was thrilled to work with Amanda Matwie for the first time, and put my book in capable, Canadian hands.

Finally, always, I need to acknowledge what my family gives up every time I approach a deadline. My kids have learned to cook for themselves because of books like this one.

And my husband...

Every second chance romance I write has a little bit of us in it. This time, it's the bickering. I love you. Let's never stop bickering, or banging, or bickering while banging. It's all so much fun.

Also by Zoe York

The books of Pine Harbour

the original series (the Minelli and Foster families)

Love in a Small Town

Love in a Snowstorm

Love on a Spring Morning

Love on a Summer Night

Love on the Run

Love in a Sandstorm

Love on the Outskirts of Town

Love on the Edge of Reason

the Kincaids of Pine Harbour

Reckless at Heart

Fierce at Heart

Wild at Heart

Fearless at Heart

Rebel at Heart

www.zoeyork.com

About the Author

Zoe York writes sexy small town romances, drawing inspiration from where she grew up just south of the Bruce Peninsula in Ontario. Since 2013, she's self-published 100 books between three pen names: she also writes spicy romance about the rich and powerful as Ainsley Booth (including sports romance), and escapist, smutty fluff as Chloe Maine. When she's not writing, she loves to travel with her husband and two sons, and her phone has nine different reading apps on it, because the dishes can wait, but the happy ever afters cannot.